WHAT TRUE LOVE IS MADE OF

Star Gazer Inn of Corpus Christi Bay, Book Five

DEBRA CLOPTON

What True Love Is Made Of

Life on Star Gazer Island and the McIntyre Ranch near Corpus Christi Texas is progressing wonderfully for Alice since finding love again and watching her sons do the same.

And now babies are on the way! Let the fun began.

But her friend Lisa hasn't been so lucky, and as happy as Alice is her heart is hurting for Lisa. But Alice is rooting for the attraction she sees between Lisa and her assistant chef, Zane.

After her horrible divorce Lisa Blair has found satisfaction being the chef at Star Gazer Inn and is delighted about everyone's newfound love. However, she had no plan about falling in love again herself, then she hired chef, Zane Tyson…and now life has become complicated. Now she's in trouble, especially after he's called out on a family emergency and might not ever return.

Zane's heart is broken after being pushed away by Lisa, the only woman he's ever loved. Now after a horrible fire, his nephew and his young wife are dead and Zane is called to their baby's side. A single man all of his life, he is now the baby's guardian and not sure how to handle it.

Now what? He's going to need help so he returns to Star Gazer Island where he knows there will be help from his friends…and maybe Alice.

Also, newly in love Tucker McIntyre and Maggie Carson are moving forward in their romance, taking it slow but steady as everyone is rooting for them.

And then all of Tucker's brothers and their wonderful wives are expecting babies…hopefully a wedding, and a baby will be in store for him and Maggie.

Don't miss this trip to Star Gazer Island…romance surrounds everyone!

CHAPTER ONE

Chef Lisa Blair stood in the garden of Star Gazer Inn, the place she loved, and was grateful to her friend Alice, the owner, for hiring her to be the chef of this great place and then taking her into partnership of the restaurant. Standing near the gate to exit out of the beautiful garden area onto the beach, she stared out at the blue topaz ocean and the soft, rolling waves. She breathed deeply, trying to stop her heart from rolling more than the waves. Trying to get a grip. She'd been trying to do this ever since her assistant chef had left town. Her heart tightened in a raw grip at calling Zane her assistant—which he had been, but he had also been more.

More that she hadn't been able to and still couldn't

embrace. Still, despite all the reasons she didn't want someone special in her life ever again, she knew Zane meant more to her than she wanted to admit.

And with good reason! Her ex-husband had totally ruined any trust she had in men when it came to relationships. She couldn't let her guard down and jump in after having been so deluded, deceived—betrayed. He'd had a sidekick, a mistress for two years before she found out. She'd hosted his lawyer parties, been his right hand and foot waitress, and put her love of becoming a chef on hold—and also her desire to become a mother—all while he'd started an affair. Only when his mistress became pregnant did he tell Lisa what he'd done and that he wanted a divorce.

How had he had a long-term affair and she not had a hint of it until he told her he was divorcing her? Was she that stupid? The question was harsh and hit her wrong, just like it did every time it slammed into her. She'd obviously been blind not to have known, seen, felt what was going on. She could never do that again— even though every part of her being told her Zane was nothing like her ex-husband Mason. And yet as hard as she tried, as hard as she wanted to accept the attraction she felt for him and what he openly felt for her, she couldn't.

And then his nephew and wife had died in a fire, and Zane had gone to rescue the tiny baby they'd saved. Even when the good man had gone to rescue this baby, he'd honored her last request to keep their relationship business related; he'd called to quit and not called her since. She'd learned details from Alice and nothing else from Zane.

Now, here she stood, looking out at this beautiful ocean she loved, feeling dead inside and lost. She had lunch to prepare and no desire to do anything but cross the grass, exit the gate, and walk to her small red house next door and close herself off from the world.

What was she supposed to do now?

~*~

Zane drove along. His nephew Dave and his beautiful, sweet wife Becca were dead…he still hadn't been able to take it all in. His heart was broken after they'd died from the fire almost a week ago now. Dave had managed to give him a call, and he'd never forget the short, barely there sound of Dave's, "I need you…"

Zane had frozen at the ragged, odd sound of Dave's voice as it rang in his ears. Dave's dad Nick, Zane's brother, had died a few years ago, and Dave's mother had died long before that. He and Dave had become close as the last of the family, and his heart had begun to thunder as Dave had continued in a rasp, "H-hospital in College Station—" and the line had gone dead.

Zane stared into the black night and rubbed his forehead as he remembered how he had scrambled from bed, thrown some clothes in a bag, and within fifteen minutes had been on the road, headed toward College Station. His heart had been pounding and his hands grasping the steering wheel with an iron grip—he'd known something terrible had happened. The few hours between him and Dave had passed quickly with the speed he had driven, but upon reaching the hospital, he learned that Dave and Becca had both passed away from fire injuries. Their home had caught fire, and Dave had gotten the baby out, then gone back in for Becca.

Evidently, it had been horrible…and now, little Nicky was left alone.

They'd left him to Zane, a chef—a single man with no children in his background…and yet they'd entrusted their precious, tiny baby boy to him.

He was honored beyond anything they could have done but he knew nothing about raising a baby. Nothing. Yes, even he couldn't deny that he was a great chef, but that had absolutely nothing to do with a baby. To say he stood on the edge of a cliff of uncertainty was putting it mildly. *What if he failed this baby?* Never in his life had he felt pressure like he did now. Thankfully, he knew where he could find help, so he was headed back home to the Corpus Christi area, to Star Gazer Island, where he knew help awaited him.

He'd moved across the bay several months ago, leaving behind a well-established restaurant he'd grown tired of being at because the owner wouldn't let him change the menu. He'd been awarded the job at Star Gazer Inn by the chef there…the beautiful, talented chef, Lisa Blair. Having terminated his job the day after learning he would be responsible for Nicky, he hadn't spoken to her since then. He'd known since their last meeting on the beach that he was going to need to quit—he shoved the thoughts of Lisa from his mind and concentrated on the road. He had a baby who needed to be his center of attention now, not a love he'd begun to feel for Lisa, only to have her turn him away. He had no time to focus on her anymore. He had this sleeping baby in the back seat of his truck who was now going to be his main focus. Making sure this baby had a happy life, memories of the mom and dad he would never remember on his own but would with help from him. He'd do his very best to honor his nephew and his lovely, sweet wife and bring this precious baby up in a happy, caring home.

Ahead of him, he saw the lights of the bridge that led over the water to Star Gazer Island. Far across the dark water, he saw the lights from the high bridge that led to Corpus Christi, a place he'd always loved. But of the two places, now more than ever, he was glad he'd bought a home on the small island and made friends with the wonderful McIntyre family. He was going to need them.

It didn't take long after coming over the bridge to turn and head down the street along the ocean's edge and to his house. He'd passed Seth and Alice's dark house; as it was one in the morning, he'd figured he'd make a quiet arrival. He hadn't wanted a lot of well-meaning friends waiting to welcome him and Nicky home. He needed to try to get a little settled in before that happened. He pulled into the carport and turned off his engine; then, glancing over his shoulder, he could tell Nicky was still sleeping. A miracle was what that was. The baby had times when he slept and times when he cried. The nurses and doctors hadn't had any trouble comforting him but since he'd left the hospital, checked into a hotel room life had been even harder since it was him trying to take care of the sweet little fella. They'd had a funeral and then met with the lawyer who read the will and Nicky had been officially left to him.

The baby had been on a roller coaster of emotions and Zane felt for sure that Nicky knew that he was not his daddy or his momma and he wanted them. At least the nurses had known how to hold him, comfort him, and make him smile. No smiles for Zane.

But he would deal with it. The nurse had kindly told him the baby would get used to him. Now, Zane was home and he quietly got out of the truck and strode to the back door and unlocked it, opened it, and turned just the lights on in the kitchen so it would give enough lights down the hallway to his room. Then he went back and, as soundlessly as possible, he released the car seat and lifted it from the back seat of the truck. After gently closing the door, he eased his way across the concrete and through the open door. He tugged the soft blanket up over Nicky's face to keep the kitchen light from waking him and then carried him into Zane's room. His hope was that the baby would sleep long enough for him to unload the baby bed and get it put together. He was going to have a rough day tomorrow with as little sleep as he was going to get, but the kid needed a bed and he was going to get it ready for him.

He set the carrier on the floor in the dark room highlighted by the kitchen light through the open door. He gently pulled the cover off Nicky's face, and his heart thundered as he took in the sweet, relaxed baby. He just stood there, fixated on the gentleness of this baby.

Get moving!

On that note, he spun, quietly pulled the door closed then went back outside, pulled his tailgate open on the truck and slid the large box onto the pavement. He quickly got it open and carried all the pieces into the room that was to be the baby's room. And there he began putting it together. It was nice, warm-toned wood. Because Nicky was a baby boy, Zane felt like this would work, but if it had been a little girl, he'd have probably chosen the white…not that that mattered.

He paused in his work, weariness sweeping over him. *Just a little more to go…*

CHAPTER TWO

Alice was going out to her car and Seth was just a few steps behind her, heading toward his truck, when she looked down the street and spotted Zane's truck in his carport.

"Zane is back. Did he tell you he was coming?" she asked Seth.

"No, he didn't tell me. Honey, he must have the baby with him because the last time I talked with him was when he said he's becoming Nicky's legal guardian."

Alice's heart pounded as she thought about the nice man who had been her second chef in charge at the inn and then had been called out because his nephew needed him. "Oh, Seth, we should go over and check on him…on them. See what he needs."

"He told me he would be coming home but never said when. They must have gotten in late last night." His expression shifted to concern as he looked from the house to her. "I know you're worried, so come on, let's go see if he's up and needs us."

Relief washed through Alice, and she grabbed her sweet husband's arm and laid her cheek against his shoulder. "Perfect. I would have been worrying all day until I knew they were okay." She smiled up at Seth, her heart warming when he kissed her forehead.

"Let's go. I'm sure he's going to need something— maybe just a loving woman to cuddle that special little boy."

Oh, how she loved this man who knew exactly what she was hoping Zane might need. She needed to cuddle the little boy who had lost his loving parents. It didn't take them but a short few moments to walk past the three houses that were between them and Zane's home. Just as they reached it, Zane opened the door, looking tired and stressed and holding a crying bundle in his arms.

"I was about to call then saw y'all coming this way

when I walked past the window. I've been trying for the last two hours to get him to calm down but nothing is working."

Alice had instantly stepped forward and reached for the baby. "Here, let me take this sweetie. Have you fed him?" She pulled the baby from his arms and cuddled him against her pounding heart. She smiled into his searching soft-green eyes. "Oh, how adorable you are, little fella. Come on now, let's calm down a bit. Let Mimi take you for a walk."

"I fed him. You already have him calmer."

She heard the weariness in the poor man's voice. She smiled at him. "I have had a little more practice than you but also, he may react better with a woman." She looked back at the baby, who was still staring at her with glistening eyes. "Get me a little bottle of water. He's got to be thirsty after all that crying."

"Good idea." Zane spun around and hurried to the counter where some baby bottles sat.

She watched as he picked up a bottle of water, twisted the top off, then turned over one of the small baby bottles on the draining board and poured a third of a bottle full of water and then put the top on and came back to her.

Alice smiled at him as she took the bottle. "You act like you know he doesn't need an entire bottle of water. That's wonderful. How did you know that?"

He hesitated—his expression clearly flustered. "I-I looked up a lot of info on my phone while in the hospital, knowing I'd be bringing him home with me. And I also asked the nurses a lot of questions. I mean, he's seven months old and eating now, and I had to get information on what to feed him. And that's when I was also told he didn't need bunches of water just yet. To be honest, that shocked me. I mean, I thought kids always need water." He sighed, and her heart squeezed for the lost look on his face as he handed her the bottle. "I'm honestly terrified that I'll do this little fella wrong. I've never had children or been around them much more than when I stopped by a table at the restaurant to ask the parents if they enjoyed the meal. What am I going to do now?"

Seth placed a hand on her shoulder and one on Zane's shoulder. "You're going to love him and ask this sweet lady lots of questions. I had no children but she's helping me be a good grandpa to little Landon, so I know she can help you." He grinned. "Zane, we are here for you, and so are all of our family members. Honestly, you're going to be a great daddy to this little man. His parents knew that, too, or they wouldn't have put you down as his protector, the one to raise him if something happened to them. They've given you a gift, and I know you're going to not let them down."

Oh, how she loved her Seth. He had a way with words, and she watched Zane take them in and then looked from Seth to his great-nephew with eyes that changed from fear to determination.

"My husband is right, and you know it. I can see it in your eyes that you are going to learn to love and cherish this sweet baby and be there for him all the way. And we will be here for both of you. Now, I'm going to rock little Nicky—do you have a rocker?"

"Not in the house, but I will get one. There's one on the back porch."

She smiled at him. "I'll take that for now, while you and Seth tend to anything you need help with." And then she headed for the back door and the beautiful porch that overlooked the water. As she settled into the seat, she realized that she might need to mention to Zane, just in case he hadn't yet thought of it, that he was going to need a fence between the boat dock and the yard. The last place he wanted this baby when he started toddling around was down on the pier and falling into that ocean. So, as she sat there and sang softly to the baby boy, she let her mind seek out things she'd need to make sure and pass over to Zane. This sweet Nicky had lost his mom and dad, but he'd been blessed with a man she knew would do everything in his power to give this little fella everything he needed.

She looked out over the shimmering water, then at the baby, whose eyes were closed, as well as his lips since he now slept in her arms. She smiled gently even as her heart hurt for him because she knew his parents had done well for the baby. They'd chosen a man who would do whatever it took to give their little love a great life.

And it hit her that maybe Zane would even eventually give him a new mother…she just hoped Lisa opened her heart before it was too late.

~*~

"So how are you?"

Seth's question the moment Alice had left the kitchen was no surprise to Zane. He looked at his friend with frank eyes. "Struggling. But you two give me hope. I know I can count on you to help me learn what I need. Still, the worry of not being enough is there. But, I'll do this—have to, for Dave and Becca."

"And you will. Now, what can I help you do?"

"Don't you have a job to get to?"

Seth pulled his phone from his pocket. "I've got a crew on this job and they know what to do. I'll call and let them know I won't be in but if they need to ask me anything, they can call. I have a feeling my hands are needed here today if what I saw in the back of your truck needs putting together. Does it?"

Relief washed over Zane. "Actually, I could use a hand. I have plenty that needs to be pulled out of boxes and put together. A stroller, a baby indoor swing, a high chair, a baby walker he slips into, and he can learn to move around—the nurses told me I would get to appreciate that because it will give him something to do while I'm working on food or house cleaning."

Seth laughed. "Well, it sounds like we have a lot to get going. And I think I saw all that same kind of stuff at Lorna and Dallas's home. And that nurse was right. Landon is walking now but he could move in that—I think they called it a baby activity walker."

Zane grinned. "Yes, that is what it is. Let's do this. Hopefully when y'all leave for the day, I'll have something he'll enjoy." And he wasn't joking. If he had to carry the little fella around all the time in order to get him to stop crying, then nothing around the house was going to get done.

Seth led the way out the door and Zane followed. But he was determined to find his way to being the daddy this little fella deserved.

CHAPTER THREE

Lisa had just dished up a salmon dish when her phone rang in her pocket. It had been a busy lunch time but it was on the slower side now. She pulled the phone out and instantly answered it when she saw it was Alice.

"Hey, is everything okay? It's not like you to suddenly not show up." She'd been told by the front desk ladies that Alice had called in and said she wouldn't be in today. Lisa had suspected that because Alice was newly married, there would be days when she decided to stay home, but she wanted to make sure she wasn't feeling bad or something.

"Everything is fine. Did you fix your special shrimp linguine alfredo today?"

"Yes, I always do on Thursdays. Why?"

"Do you still have enough for three plates?"

What was going on? "Yes. Do you want it?"

"Yes, actually, I do. And I waited until after the lunch rush to see if you could deliver it to us. And if you want to join us, make it four orders."

"Do you have company?"

"Umm, no. Actually, we are Zane's company. The poor man drove most of the night and has been working all morning. We need food, so please help us out and come to his home. Thanks, see you soon."

"Wait—" she yelped, but the line was dead. *What was Alice doing?* She wanted to call her back and tell her she was not coming over there, but she knew she was going. She had to see Zane and the baby and help out if there was anything she could do. And taking them lunch was something Alice knew she wouldn't—no, couldn't not do. She inhaled a deep breath and let it out slowly, hoping to ease her racing, rushing blood flow. And then she told the assistants to take over, that she had four plates to get ready and to deliver to Alice.

And then she went to work. Alice knew this was a

meal that was cooked all morning and would be easy to get ready quickly. Her boss, her friend, had planned this on purpose. And as she walked out of the inn with her load, she couldn't help but be glad Alice had made this move. She knew doing it this way gave Lisa no way out and helped her be able to at least see Zane and his new baby.

When she drove up to the house, she pulled into the drive and parked behind his truck. There were a lot of empty boxes in the back of the truck, and instantly she wondered what they were doing. As she pulled the large bag of food from the back seat of her car and then walked past the truck, she saw one of the boxes had a baby swing on the front. *They were putting baby things together.* She knocked on the door and could hear them talking, so she opened the door and stepped inside the kitchen just as Zane came out of the hallway.

He stopped the moment he saw her.

Heart pounding, she tried to get control of herself. "I brought lunch." She lifted the bag up.

He stepped forward as if realizing he had just been standing there, staring at her. "Thanks. Let me relieve you of that."

His hand touched hers as he wrapped his finger around the handles of the bag and slipped his other hand under the bag to help support it, and she slid her hand out from under his warm touch. Her hand shook slightly as she quickly crossed her arms and tucked her hands beneath her upper arms. He held her gaze for a second, then walked away from her and set the bag on the counter.

So, it was going to be uncomfortable between them. She'd done this, pushed him away and ignored the kiss they'd shared that last night on the beach. True, when he'd come to check on her, she had fumbled her words, paused, and given him the idea that she wanted him to kiss her, and he'd jumped on the chance. She'd instantly been drawn into his embrace and the feel of his lips against her. There was a need to be closer to him and the deep want to let herself need him, want him, and in doing so let him have control of her…something she could not and would not ever give a man the power to have over her. So, she'd broken from the life-changing kiss and finished saying what she'd been trying to say.

Told him she could never have a relationship with him and only wanted him to work for her and not have any personal relationship. He'd looked stunned and then he'd left, and the next two weeks of work had been terrible with the strain between them.

Then he'd gotten the call about his family's tragedy, quit work, and now here he stood, a guardian…a stand-in-daddy for his nephew's beloved baby. Her heart ached for him because she knew how much everything about the situation hurt him. One thing she'd figured out about Zane was that other than being a well-known and respected chef, he seemed alone. Especially now, since he'd lost his nephew.

She reined in her runaway thoughts. "I'm so sorry all this happened to your family. How can I help?"

"There's nothing you need to do—"

"Lisa, you made it," Alice exclaimed as she also came from around the corner where Zane had entered from. "Here, come see this sweet baby boy. He just went to sleep but you can see how adorable he is, bless his sweet heart." Alice must have sensed the troubled atmosphere because she strode across the room and linked her arm around Lisa's right arm and led her toward the back, just as Seth rounded the corner, carrying a box.

"Good to see you, Lisa. Can't wait to eat what you've brought us."

"I hope you like it."

"I like anything you cook."

"He really does," Alice said. "Now, y'all get it ready. I'm showing Lisa the baby. We'll be right back."

"Will do." Seth grinned. "He's a cutie and already stole our hearts, so get ready."

Her heart pounded as they went down the hall and entered a bedroom that had the beginnings of a lot of useful baby items. But the main one was the brown baby bed that Alice led her over to. And there he lay on his back, his arms spread wide as he seemed to be calling to her to hug him. She pushed the sudden overwhelming need to reach for him and cuddle him close. *What was she thinking?*

"Isn't he the perfect baby boy?"

Lisa swallowed, trying to put moisture back into her throat so she could speak. "Y-yes, he is."

"One day, he and my little Landon will be buddies and then all my sweet new grandbabies who are on the way. He's perfect. And my heart aches for the loss of his parents, but I'm so happy he has Zane." Alice looked at Lisa, and she felt her gaze, so she looked at her friend, who continued talking. "He's going to be a great daddy, a guardian with a huge heart to give this boy." Her words were all whispered so not to wake the child, or maybe so they wouldn't roll along the hallway into the kitchen where Zane was. "Don't you agree?"

Lisa tore her gaze from Alice and put them back on the precious sleeping baby boy. "Yes, even though he lost his parents, he's been blessed to have Zane in his life." And she heartfully believed it. The baby was precious. Oh, how she'd always wanted babies of her own. But her backstabbing, affair-having ex-husband had taken that dream away. Not even thinking, she reached into the bed and gently touched the dark baby hair and her heart ached. She pulled her fingers away and stepped from the bed. "They are probably waiting on you." She turned and walked out the door.

"Wait, aren't you eating with us?"

She'd brought a meal but knew now she couldn't do it. "I—"

"Hey, it's ready, ladies," Seth said from where he stood at the back door. "We have it set up on the porch, so come on before the baby wakes up. You did good, Lisa. It looks and smells delicious."

"Come on, don't leave." Alice smiled at her. "There is a baby back there who is going to need all of us." She raised her eyebrows.

"Okay, lead the way," she said, and tossed her worries deep into the pit that churned in her stomach. This moment wasn't about her or her feelings; it was about a baby who had a new life to get used to, and she knew that above all else, that needed to be taken to heart. Her heart didn't count right now.

~*~

Zane was trying not to be upset with Seth and Alice for having Lisa deliver the meal and for having invited her to stay. He'd been set up by the two who had saved him this morning with the baby and setting up all the gear.

Being mad at this would be childish, so he fought it down hard as he watched Lisa take the seat beside him at the table for four that Seth held out for her before pulling out his wife's chair for her. He should have stood and pulled out Lisa's chair but he hadn't done it; despite how he was feeling about her being there, he felt bad that he'd remained sitting.

"So this is still warm and smells great," he said, not really sure where to go with conversation while she was here.

"I hope you like it, everyone." She picked up her fork and dipped it into the noodles and shrimp, then took the large bite immediately.

He did the same, almost chuckling at her deliberate way of ending their conversation with a forkful of food. He caught the look that passed between Seth and Alice before they did the same, and thankfully the next few minutes were silent as a swallow got immediately replaced with another bite.

"So, are you going to put the baby in daycare or get someone to come to the house and take care of him while you go back to work?" Alice asked after several bites and sips of iced tea.

"I'm not going back to work. I'm going to devote all my time to Nicky. He needs that. I thought you understood that when I called and resigned." He said the last words to Lisa.

She blinked, then put her fork down. "I knew you weren't coming back. It was Alice who asked you that question, not me."

They stared at each other, and he knew he should have kept his mouth shut. There was too much churning between them.

"I was just asking. So, you're going to be a full-time dad?" Alice asked.

"Yes." He set his fork down now, knowing he had to get a hold of himself. "And I'm not his dad. Dave was his dad and was a wonderful dad and was going to be amazing as he brought this baby up." Unable to sit any longer, he rose to his feet and turned toward the water. "I've listened to every piece of advice you have given me, and it's helped me tremendously. But it's just going to take time for me to grow secure with the treasure I am now responsible for." He turned back to them. "So yes,

I'm staying home and giving that boy everything I have to give him."

Seth nodded, looking as if he totally understood, and Alice got up and came over and hugged him. "We're here for you, but you are going to be wonderful. I'm going to go check on your little fella."

Lisa stood as Seth got up and gathered the plates. "I'll carry those in."

"No, I've got this. Thanks for bringing it."

He stacked them on top of each other then entered the screen door, pulling it open with one hand while balancing the plates, and then letting it close behind him.

Leaving Zane alone with Lisa.

Zane's heart thundered in his chest, and he wanted to punch it as he met Lisa's gaze.

"I'll be going. Zane, I know I didn't say what you hoped on our last meeting out there by the ocean but, if you need me, I'll be here. Anything I can do to help you and that darling little fella you've been blessed with through such a sad loss...I'll be here to help." She started to head toward the sidewalk that led around to the carport and her car; then, she paused. "You're going to be a wonderful second father to Nicky. He's blessed to have you." She held his gaze with her beautiful soft-green eyes.

Heart pounding harder, he forced words from his lips. "Thank you. I…may call you sometime…if Nicky needs something."

"Okay. Just remember, I've never had a baby or been around many, but I would try very hard to help. That sweet baby deserves everything you and all of us can give him. Bye."

He watched her turn and head away from him, and he forced his feet to stay exactly where they were. If they weren't going to be together like he'd wanted, at least she was trying to help. *Could he try to get hold of himself and just be her friend?*

Especially since Nicky was the one who was going to need, and get, all of his attention from here on out.

CHAPTER FOUR

Lisa had gone back to the kitchen and had been cooking all afternoon. Even if she had no orders, she was testing new recipes—intent on keeping her hands and mind busy. She also complimented her staff, telling them how great they were doing and how valuable they were to the restaurant and to her. It was true. Seeing Zane had reminded her immensely of their value, especially after losing his talent here in her kitchen. She talked, basically nonstop, the entire afternoon. And it was necessary, or she would have been standing over there at the grill, fuming, and she needed to get her emotions out in a positive way. She needed to concentrate on her work…her work had saved her over and over again through the ordeals of her life.

Now, she had more than she knew how to handle: Zane and his new baby, the pain he was going through, the absolute rejection he obviously felt from her—which was her fault. Even though at the lunch today she'd tried pitifully to undo it, she knew she had lost that battle. *And why was she even trying when she knew deep down she couldn't just be friends with Zane? Would she ever get control of the emotions that man pulled from her?*

And Alice…what was Alice trying to do? Ruin their friendship? She rubbed her forehead—she knew that wasn't what her friend was trying to do. Her friend was trying to help her in some way, yet Lisa didn't want that kind of help. *Could Alice not see that?*

"Miss Lisa, are you okay?" Lilly asked.

Lisa looked up from where she was grilling a steak. Lilly was a beautiful young lady, single, and as far as Lisa knew, she didn't date much. She was always willing to work as much as Lisa needed her, and lately she had stepped in to take up the void left by Zane's leaving. She'd been working for her for a while now and had a great talent, a promising talent of cooking and getting plates together.

"I'm fine. I mean, I'm talking, right?"

Lilly's expression was soft, concerned. "Yes, but you don't normally talk so much, so I was wondering if something was…wrong. To be truthful, when something is bothering me, I tend to talk too much—well, not too much. You're not talking too much more than you normally do. No one else has probably even noticed. But, well, I watch you. I think you are amazing, and I may study you closer than I need to because I'm really wanting to become as talented as you. So, anyway, I can hush. I was just reaching out in case you needed something."

Lisa's heart clenched. This young woman was really nice, and she was often quiet and so was she, usually. She wondered whether everyone else had noticed her difference or whether Lilly had noticed it simply because they were similar. Lisa had noticed how similar she and this young woman were and how hard she was working to become a great chef one day. She did have the talent, and Lisa was sure she would reach her goal one day.

"It's okay. I do have something on my mind—you read me right. And thank you for reaching out to me. It means a lot to me, but I don't think I should or need to talk about it right now. So let's get some good meals out there to these great customers." She looked back at the grill. "Oh, I better not burn this steak." She flipped it over immediately. Yes, she needed to focus on the food, but she really appreciated Lilly reaching out to her. Lisa would make certain that she taught this young woman everything she could as she was stepping in right now helping with Zane's absence, and for that, Lisa wanted to help her succeed. Lilly had gladly stepped up to help take some of the strain off Lisa's shoulders. It helped Lisa, at least here in the kitchen since her strains far outreached the kitchen area now. It was far deeper and far, far more troublesome than cooking meals for everyone.

~*~

The evening breeze off the ocean was cool tonight. Tucker McIntyre was glad he had Maggie Carson in his life and they'd decided to eat out tonight. They sat on the restaurant patio of his mother's inn and had already ordered their meal; now they were just enjoying the scenery, his being Maggie. The weather could be horrible and if she were sitting beside him, it would still be a great day.

She pulled her gaze from the horizon and smiled. "Your mom did a wonderful thing when she opened Star Gazer Inn. And you can look around and see everyone sitting out here is enjoying themselves."

He loved hearing the joy in Maggie's words. He reached for her hand and gently held it on the table between them. "Yeah, her deciding to reopen the inn was a great move on her part. We were worried about her after Dad died but opening the inn helped her find herself again. It's been great for her and it helped a lot of people. If it hadn't been for Mom opening the inn, my brother Jackson might never have met Nina. And it could have been the same way for Dallas and Lorna. Saving her on the beach and being there for her while she gave birth to Landon might never have happened. And now Mom has a grandson she instantly claimed in

Landon and is expecting more. Lots of cool things have happened since the inn opened." He ran his finger along her thumb.

Her pretty eyes studied him. "It seems that way."

"The best part is that if Nina hadn't married my brother and then talked you into moving here, I might never have met you. I have to say, Star Gazer Inn is a magical place for me." He loved watching the way she took in what he said, her eyes so soft and expressive and the touch of a smile lifting at the beautiful corners of her mouth. It gave him hope that they would have that happy ending that all his family were having since the inn opened.

"It all kind of makes me wonder if other people who've come to stay at the inn have had experiences. You know, did their love deepen or if they were not here with someone special, did they meet someone here? I've started believing that Star Gazer Inn might be a special place where new love makes a beginning or old love revives."

She squeezed his hand and her smile bloomed big. "Tucker McIntyre, you, I think, are a romantic. That would be pretty cool. Although I have to point out to you that we didn't meet here at the inn. But it has been a joy every time we've come here for dinner."

"You're right. Thankfully, my sister-in-law moved you in out on the ranch next door to me. But...if she hadn't met my brother here and fallen in love with him, then you would have never been in that cabin next to mine. This would never have happened. I'm still thinking the inn had something to do with our love story. My mom would like to think that, too. She loves the fact that after she reopened this inn where she and my dad met all those years ago, she met Seth. Love has been in the air."

"This is a side of you that I haven't seen, and it makes me love you more."

He wanted to lean over the table and take her lips in his. He loved this woman. Loved her so much. He would, if he had to, wait on her forever to make the decision to marry him. He would do whatever he had to do...just having her sitting here across the table from him was a huge joy. Having her in his arms and in his life as his wife...he could never be happier if that happened. But right now, he just wanted to be what she needed. To be here for her as she, as he had, worked through the pain and loss of her first love. His mom had done it and Seth had waited for her. And Tucker would wait for Maggie.

"There's Lisa, and she looks a little disturbed." Maggie looked over his shoulder, toward the ocean.

He turned and saw Lisa, the chef of this great place, coming into the garden through the gate that led out to the beach. He knew she was probably having some trouble since Zane had left town.

"I bet she's really busy since Zane isn't here anymore."

"She has help though, right?" Concern filled Maggie's voice.

"Yes, Mom said she does."

"Speaking of your mom, I haven't seen her. She usually comes and gives us a hug. You know, she likes it when we come—she likes it when any of her sons and their wives come."

He looked around. "You're right. I don't know where Mom is. That's odd." He watched Lisa walk through the small gate onto the dining room outdoor patio. They were close enough that he softly said her name. "Lisa, how are you?"

She paused, turning to look at him with disturbed eyes, as if she hadn't even known they were there.

Worry for her escalated in that moment.

"Oh, hi. I'm fine. I-I didn't see y'all. It's nice to see you both. I think my-my helpers are probably needing me." She turned to go.

"Wait." He wasn't letting her go yet. She'd rambled the last couple of sentences, she was so sidetracked or troubled. Something wasn't right. "Are you okay?"

She glanced around and then stepped closer to them, as if to make sure no one else could hear their conversation. "I'm fine. I've, you know, just had to get used to Zane not being here and started training the two girls I've stepped up into sub-chef positions since he quit. They are very good, and I probably should have raised them up the ladder sooner. It gives me a little bit more time to be out of the kitchen, like your mother suggested early on. I just needed to make sure the food was right…but sometimes I just need a little bit of a break, so both of them work beside me and are really great."

"I understand." Maggie reached out and touched Lisa's arm. "There has been a lot of strain on you, running the chef position alone of this wonderful, delicious kitchen. Then suddenly losing your right-hand chef had to be hard. But you're great—at least, everything I've seen since moving here says you are. You are a very organized, awesome business-running person. It probably helped him, knowing you could handle it, and enabled him to rescue this sweet baby. Have you heard from him?"

"Um…" she stuttered and looked at Tucker. "You haven't talked to your mom today?"

"No, I haven't. None of my brothers said anything about talking to her either. Is she not here? We just noticed we hadn't seen her yet and usually she comes out immediately and hugs us and welcomes us."

"Zane got home late last night. And this morning, she and Seth saw his truck and they went over and saw the new baby. They took the day off so she could take care of Nicky, and Seth could help Zane put things together. You know, strollers and baby walkers so he can learn to push with his little feet and legs before walking. He'd picked up a lot of baby things before heading home. Then they called me right after lunch and asked me to bring them some meals, so I did, then I came back to work. I just assumed she'd let you all know what was going on."

It was easy to see she was not herself. He glanced at Maggie, and her eyes told him she was as disturbed as he was by the look on Lisa's face and the uncertainty of her voice. He looked back at the stressed-out chef and family friend. "We haven't gotten a call from her but I believe after we eat, we'll run by there and check on them. Thanks for telling us and thanks for taking the lunch. How's the baby doing?"

Lisa crossed her arms and gave him a small smile that was semi-fake…not her usually open smile. "He was great. I just saw him for a few moments when I arrived because your mom had just put him down to nap. Then we all sat on the porch and ate—they'd had me bring myself a meal also. But he hadn't awakened before I left, so I'd barely seen him. But he looks adorable. I don't think he's walking yet and that's why all those cute baby toys. One was a little four-legged carrier with wheels and a seat in the middle for the baby. He'll be wheeling around in that soon, I'm sure. He'll have a big choice, it looked like, from what Zane had picked up. He looked tired when I saw him from the long drive."

Tucker had no doubt after hearing her and watching her that part of her problem was Zane. His mom had told him that there was something between these two.

"Well, I need to go check on the kitchen. Hopefully when y'all go visit them, everything is still good."

He watched her walk away. Questions bounced inside his brain as he looked over at Maggie. "That…I don't—that was confusing."

"Very. I think she cares for Zane. And well, maybe something is wrong between them. I mean, she doesn't have any children, does she?"

"No, not that I've ever known about. She was married to that jerk for years and then he left her for a woman he'd been having an affair with for two years while Lisa hosted and cooked for all of his business parties. And only after the mistress got pregnant and he told Lisa he was divorcing her did she even know about the affair. It was a ridiculous tale, and I was hoping, and I know Mom is hoping she finds real, true love. Mom said she'd wanted a baby but he'd kept putting it off as his law firm grew and Lisa had to keep putting off her dream of becoming a mom. By the time they split, she was nearly fifty-two."

Maggie reached across the table and took his hand again. "I feel for her. I hate bad romance stories. I was blessed with a wonderful love of my life until Mark died. And I never even imagined after losing him that I'd get blessed with a second love story until you came into my life. Thank you. I'm going to pray for her. You know, that maybe with as much emotion as she's showing that something is going on in her heart. And that baby just lost his mom and dad—so terrible, but maybe God is giving him a blessing and Zane is going to need help."

Tucker loved this woman, and he squeezed her soft hand, one of the hands that typed fast on her computer, creating love stories for people to get lost in. He'd gotten lost in her. "I have to say, that is a great idea. I know that you loving me is a great idea and I'm grateful. For Zane and Lisa, that would be cool but I don't know…something just seems off."

"Maybe so. But you and I both know that things can be overcome. I'm so glad we came tonight. And I'm looking forward to talking to your mom in a bit and seeing that baby."

"Well, hang on to that thought because here comes our food and as soon as we get finished, we are heading over there." And he meant it. *Why had his mom not called them?* They'd all been worried about that baby, and she should have called. Yep, something was up and he planned to find out what. He'd really hated seeing the pain in Lisa's eyes. At least he and Maggie had known love before losing them but Lisa hadn't, and it hurt, seeing her look so distraught.

CHAPTER FIVE

Zane carried a wide-awake little Nicky in his arms as he walked Alice and Seth out to the driveway. The sun had set and it was dark, but their road had the light of the moon and like his house, many of them along the road had a lamplight near the road. His day had been full but he felt better after having had this great couple help him out in getting ready to start out right.

"Thank you both for staying with me all day. Alice, you did great with this little fella and helped me get a grip on how to carry him around and feeding rituals. You were awesome. Look at him, how content he is. He looks totally happy right now—that might change after you leave but I'll take your advice on how to deal with those moments. And Seth, you were a big help to me. I thank you both."

They both smiled at him. Seth, as always, clapped a hand on his shoulder and held on. "You are going to be a good daddy and are going to make that couple proud that they left their boy to you." There was a tremble in his voice as he spoke that Zane didn't miss. "I never had any kids. My sweet wife couldn't have any and then she got cancer later on…and passed away. So now that I've fallen for this beautiful woman, I've adopted her wonderful family as my own. When all of the grandbabies come along, I'm going to love them greatly. And I can tell you that couple picked you because they love you, and they know you will do what this baby needs. And I have a feeling they also knew this sweet baby can do a lot for you. In reality, you are like I was—I had no one but my first wife, and I lost her, and you had no one but this baby's parents and him. So, we are here for you. Okay?"

"Yeah, I really appreciate you both. And I'm going to be as good of a daddy as I can be and work very hard at it."

Alice stepped up to him and placed a hand on the

baby's arm and one on his shoulder. "You're going to be a great daddy. And I've enjoyed being here today and will be here every day you need me because I have plenty of help at the inn who can take my place. But you have others out there willing to help you…so if you aren't calling me all the time, I certainly understand. Now, you two have a good night." She leaned back from him, and then stood on her tiptoes and kissed him on the cheek. "You are a wonderful man, Zane, and just like my sweet husband said, this baby is going to do well with you as his father. His parents were very smart putting you into that spot. Knowing if something happened to them that this little fella would be cherished and well looked after. Good night. Call us if you need us."

Zane watched them head down the driveway, arm in arm. A wonderful couple who had started a new life. A couple who he had been envying there for a little while. Just as they reached the driveway, a truck pulled up. He immediately recognized it as Tucker's. They stopped walking and Tucker grinned at him through the open window. Zane could see Maggie, hopefully his soon-to-be bride, watching him from the passenger seat.

Tucker glanced at his mom and Seth. "We went to eat at the inn and we heard this rumor that you were back in town and had the baby with you, and that Mom and Seth were over here, helping you out. So we came to check things out. Looks like she was right. Can we get out and take a look at him?"

He knew exactly who they had talked to, and his thoughts immediately went where he didn't want them to go…straight to Lisa. "Yeah, come on and get out. He's awake and would be happy to see some new people and get a little entertainment from you. Although I need to tell you, I've put your mom and your—" What did they call Seth now, the man who'd taken the place of their dad? *Dad? Father? Stepdad*—no, that wouldn't work. *Seth?* He was confused.

Tucker climbed out of the truck; Maggie was already out and rounding the end of the truck, smiling at the baby. Seth looked from her back to Tucker, who was grinning.

"He calls me Seth," Seth said as he plopped his hand on Tucker's shoulder now. "I'm not taking the place of his dad but hopefully I'm in a good spot and he can call me anything he wants to. Who knows, he might call me Pops or something like that, but Seth is fine with me."

Tucker grinned. "Yeah, he's Seth to me and that's what I call him. But he's my sweet mom's husband and closer to me than most fellas. Now, what's this little fella going to call you? He is cute."

Maggie held her arms out. "While y'all are talking, can I hold him?"

He grinned at her because she looked overwhelmingly excited. "Sure you can." Zane handed Nicky over to her, and she instantly cuddled him and started talking to him. She tickled his chin with her pointer finger and the tip of his nose as she cooed and teased him.

Everybody watched her, enthralled. She looked like a mom herself. *She wasn't even marri—* Zane halted his thoughts. He'd almost said she wasn't even married yet, but she had been married and this was probably one of the things, besides her husband, that had been taken away from her when he'd been in that car wreck and killed.

"You're good with him," he said gently, meaning it, and everyone agreed. He looked over at Tucker and saw a lot of emotion in the eyes of his friend.

She looked up at all of them, smiling. "Yes, I wrote happily-ever-after books, married the man I loved, and dreamed of babies. He's adorable." Her gaze settled on Tucker.

Tucker moved closer to her, put his arm across her shoulders, and leaned in to play with the baby too.

They were a great-looking couple. Zane looked over at Alice and knew what she was seeing between her son and this sweet lady was hope for her son. That these two who had lost so much would realize they were meant for each other. Zane hoped so too.

His thoughts once again shifted over to Lisa. Lisa, who did not want him. Lisa, who had made it clear that she didn't want to commit to anything or take a risk with anyone, making sure that no one else could do to her what her lousy ex-husband had done. *It was heart-wrenching that she even put him in the same category with that creep. Maddening—* He yanked his thoughts from those and focused on the beautiful scene in front of him.

"I'm going to have him here at the house. I'm not going to be working. I'm going to be devoting my time to raising him. But, you look like you have a way with babies and enjoy them. Since you're going to be just one street over, if you ever want to come keep him while I run a few errands, I could call you."

A smile took over Maggie's entire face and her eyes glistened. "You call me any time. It would be a blessing to step in and help you and this little sweetie out. But I'm sure you're going to have a lot of offers, so don't ever feel like you have to call me. I totally understand."

He wasn't sure who all she was talking about, but he knew that Alice was standing here and had a bunch of great daughters-in-law, so he had a feeling she was right, he would have plenty of help. "Yeah, I moved here at the right time. Because if I still lived over the bridge in Corpus, I wouldn't have all you great people around me. So, thanks from my heart."

He spent the next few minutes watching the young couple playing with his new son and hope filled him. He'd misspoken, because moving to Star Gazer Island had been a great decision. It was as if he was supposed to be here in this pleasant place for this little fella.

~*~

Maggie looked at the table on her back patio that she'd decorated for lunch for all the friends who were coming to see her and her new home today. Lorna, Sophie, and Nina—they'd all agreed to come for lunch and were excited to see her new house. She was so thrilled that as much as she loved Tucker and his brothers, she loved his sisters-in-law very much, too. They each matched their husbands perfectly: Nina to Jackson, Lorna to Dallas, and Sophie to Riley. Tucker was the only one without a mate and she hoped she matched him as well as the others matched his brothers. The thought had her pausing and thinking about last night, holding that sweet baby with him standing close. It had touched her soul deeply and had her heart churning with want for what she could have with him by her side. *But was she ready?* That question held her back.

She just hadn't yet been able to commit to anything, but she was so glad to have this new cottage here on wonderful Star Gazer Island and just about twenty miles down the road from Tucker and his family's huge ranch, where she'd met him. She hadn't regretted moving here. And next week, she and Tucker were going back to her home there in the Dallas area and were going to get her things ready to move. She was looking forward to that, never having thought she could do it. After losing her beloved husband in that horrible wreck, she had never imagined that she would move from the home that they had loved together and where so many precious memories of them were stored…but it was time.

And today she was having lunch for all the women who had been so wonderful to her since she'd come here. Taking a deep breath of contentment, she looked out at the ocean. It was calm today and with the sun sparkling on the blue waters, the wonder of how it would be in the next few months popped into her thoughts suddenly. *What was it like in the Corpus area in the next months as the fall moved into Texas? Would it be cold here, cool, or remain warm?* It was something she'd never thought about before. In the Plano area on the outskirts of Dallas, it would get cold enough for sleet, freezes, and some snow. Here, she didn't feel like that would be a problem, and she liked the idea.

She heard a car turn in to the drive, so, tucking her hair behind her ears, she hurried across the patio and down the sidewalk, then around the edge of the house and through the carport, where Nina's SUV had now parked. The engine went off and the doors swung open as all three ladies stepped out. Nina and Lorna were both expecting around Christmas—one right before and one right after—so Christmas was going to hold wonderful excitement this year for the family. She was so delighted that she'd be around for it.

"I'm so glad all of you could come out. Nina and Lorna, both of you have great little bumps now. How exciting. Aren't y'all glad to finally be showing?"

Nina chuckled as she rubbed her little protruding belly. "I am thrilled. And he's starting to move! When he starts today, I'll let y'all know and maybe everyone can feel the little sweetie kicking me." She laughed at her words, as did everyone.

"Mine is kicking me some too." Lorna chuckled. "Isn't it wonderful?"

"Yes, it is." Nina grinned with satisfaction, and Maggie felt a touch of jealousy—oh, how she had looked forward to these types of moments for herself.

Sophie came up to Maggie and draped an arm around her shoulders. "I'm not pregnant, but me and Riley are giving it every chance we can to get a baby to come into this world with us as soon as possible. I never thought I'd be saying that so soon after marrying the man of my dreams, but you know I'm not a baby myself anymore and it's time. I'm so ready to love and hold our baby. Our baby will be a camping or rodeo boy or girl. Don't you think?"

Everyone laughed at her words, because Riley was a cowboy like all his brothers but had also opened the camp on their ranch's beach property, and that was where he and Sophie had fallen in love.

"It's all wonderful," Maggie said. "Absolutely wonderful. Okay, let's get this party going. Hopefully y'all will enjoy lunch—I never said I was the greatest cook in the world but I do enjoy it. And in all honesty, I haven't cooked much in a long while, so I needed practice and thought you great gals would be good test subjects."

Everyone was laughing at her joke as they rounded

the corner of the house—and stopped and stared at the view. She glanced at them as some looked at the new outside table she'd just bought. It was round, light-brown wood with wooden chairs that weren't too heavy to move around but wouldn't blow away if the wind picked up. She placed beautiful pads on the seats and the backs that were the merging colors of an evening sunset over the waters: soft blues, gentle orange, and pale pink merging together. In the middle of the table, she'd placed a flower arrangement with similar colors, and she'd put out all of her new glassware that had similar tones as the water. Her plates did also and went well with the new silverware beside them. Yes, she had plenty of glasses and plates back home that she was going to bring here, things with lots of memories, things she loved, but she was also buying new things, things that could help her remember and know that it was time to move forward. That it was time to start over.

And it was. Memories, wonderful memories, were there but it was time for a new start, and it had all began when Nina had called her and talked her into coming here to their ranch and staying in a small cabin and starting back to writing her books. It had been a miracle that she'd needed and among that miracle she'd met Tucker. As thoughts whirled through her mind, she realized they were all quiet as they looked from her patio out to the water.

"Okay, so what do you ladies think?"

Nina looked at her. "It's perfect and, girlfriend, you can practice on me anytime as long as I get to enjoy this view."

"Thanks." She smiled then glanced at Sophie and Lorna, who looked at her with wide eyes.

"It's beautiful." Lorna touched her shoulder. "I'm a little jealous. I'm going to be honest—I'm on the ranch, so I don't have a view of the ocean, but this is just amazing. And you've matched it up so perfectly."

"You're welcome to come here any time you want to."

"Thank you very much. I might take you up on that sometime."

"I agree with them," Sophie said. "But this makes me happy that Riley and I have started building our house on the beach land near the camp, so we will also have an ocean view. But this is beautiful, two different views. I bet at night it's cool because you can see out there across the bay the lights of Corpus Christi."

"Yes, it is one of the things I love. I'm just glad to be here. Glad I found it that morning before anyone else saw it and bought it. Now, I'm going to make Star Gazer Island my new home. Now, Lorna and Nina, you two sit down. Me and Sophie will bring the casserole and salad out to you two expecting moms." She beamed.

Sophie grinned. "She's right. You two sit down, and I'll help her. This is going to be a fun day."

Lorna looked at Nina; they hitched their brows, then pulled out their chairs and sat.

"Fine, have it your way, you two, and we aren't going to feel the least bit guilty about being waited on." Nina rubbed her tummy as she winked at Lorna.

Maggie and Sophie smiled, then headed for the house.

As soon as the door closed behind them, Maggie grinned at Sophie. "Are they both doing good?"

"Nina is having more morning sickness than Lorna has shown, but you did good getting her to sit down. I must tell you that Riley said you buying this house and staying here has made Tucker so happy. He's been different the last few days, and we are all noticing."

A warm rush of happiness raced through Maggie as she picked up the dish of chicken cordon bleu casserole, and her thoughts went to last night with him and holding the baby. "I'm so glad I met him…Sophie, I love him, and I never thought I could love someone again. And he feels the same way."

Sophie picked up the bowl of salad. "I've never been in love with anyone until Riley, so I can't even imagine how I would feel if I lost him. You and Tucker know how that feels, so we are all ecstatic for you both."

Her heart squeezed. "Thank you. Not only did coming here help me find my new way forward, I found Tucker and all of you. Now, let's go eat this while it's warm. Thankfully, the dressing and the iced tea is already out there."

"Can't wait to try that dish you are carrying."

"I love it and was ready to have some finally, so I made it for y'all."

They went back onto the porch and each took a seat

at the round table after they set their dishes down. They all got some and chatted as they did. Everyone loved the casserole instantly, which made Maggie happy. She might not own a restaurant but had always loved to cook.

Nina took a drink of her tea, then set the blue glass back on the table. "Okay, so you're going next week to load up and then you'll officially be a resident of Star Gazer Island. Tucker's going to help you move your things, isn't he?"

"Yes. You ladies have a wonderful brother-in-law, and I'm sure you all know that. He's going to help me move here and has agreed to move slowly on our relationship. This is a wonderful place and the perfect place for me to start over. I know each of you have gone through hardships and have either overcome it or learned to adjust and come to live with it. That's where I am. And wonderful Tucker totally understands, because he's been through losing his love too. So, we're going to travel this road together and when the time is right, I hope that we have more.

"But, in the meantime, we're going to bring some

of my things that I loved between me and Mark here, because I don't want to forget him. I want to start a new life with his wonderful memories and his urging me forward into my new life. And Tucker is the same way with his memories of Darla after she was taken away from him. So he's going with me to help me as I go through all my things and set my road forward in motion." Her heart pounded hard in her chest as her sweet friends took in her words.

Nina lifted her glass of tea in the air. "Let's have a toast." Instantly, everyone lifted their glasses of tea and Maggie did also as her friend smiled gently at her. "To forward in motion…may it be a beautiful road, full of joy and more wonderful memories to add to those you carry with you." She smiled and then everyone clinked their glasses together, eyes twinkling at Maggie as they took a sip.

Her heart thundered watching them. She was here, home, and she was going to start over, a life full of memories and more to make of the two men she loved: Mark and now Tucker.

Her thoughts went again to holding that precious

baby, and it hit her suddenly that no one had mentioned the new baby coming to town. "Have y'all—" she said suddenly. "Have y'all heard about Alice and Seth going over to welcome the baby to town? Tucker and I heard about it at the inn's restaurant yesterday evening and went straight over after we finished eating. They were all on the driveway as Alice and Seth were leaving, so we stopped to see the baby. He's just adorable. I got to hold him, and it was wonderful." Only then did she realize everyone looked at her with startled expressions.

Nina was first. "What baby? Are you talking about the one Zane went to check on? The one who lost his parents in the fire?"

"Yes, sorry. I got to hold him, and it was wonderful. I assumed all of you had heard since he had arrived. Though it was late the night before when Zane and the baby got into town." *Why had she expected this when Tucker hadn't heard?* She'd assumed that somehow he had been the only one who hadn't known.

Everyone looked at one another.

"We haven't heard this," Sophie said. "Obviously, our husbands haven't heard either or we would have known."

"How did y'all find out?" Lorna leaned forward in her chair. "At the restaurant at the inn?"

"Yes. We went to eat, and your mother-in-law wasn't there. We saw Lisa coming in from the beach, and she looked distracted. We wondered what was wrong and called her over. She was the one who told us, and I think that's why she looked as shocked as I am looking at y'all because she'd thought we would have heard from Alice that Zane and the baby had arrived. So, I'm still in shock that y'all don't know."

Nina rubbed her forehead. "Obviously, for some reason, Alice hasn't told us. I wonder what's up with that?"

Sophie tapped her fingernails on the table. "Okay, maybe she's waiting on the guys to get to the ranch and maybe get them all together to tell them. But that can't be right; they don't all go to the ranch each morning like they used to when Alice was at the house. I would have thought she'd be calling to let us know since we were all concerned for Zane and the baby. I'm the newest into the family and find this so odd, don't y'all?"

"Yes," Nina agreed.

Lorna nodded slowly. "But you know, now that I think about it, Dallas, who is at our ranch now in the morning, got a call from someone to come to the ranch. So, he was going over to see what the meeting was about. So maybe you're right, their mom had driven over there to tell them all at the same time. But why?"

It was strange, and that was all Maggie could think. Or maybe Tucker was involved. Maybe he saw something last night that she missed. Or maybe after he dropped her off, he and his mom talked and he learned something that called for the silence. She suddenly felt as if she shouldn't have said anything, so she kept those thoughts to herself and watched all those she was now starting to think of as her sisters-in-law contemplate what was going on. And then suddenly phones were out, and calls were being made.

And all because she'd opened her mouth.

CHAPTER SIX

Two days after he and Nicky had arrived home, Zane needed to go to the grocery store. He had that night he'd headed back to Star Gazer and he'd bought enough to get by with for a few days, but he needed to replenish. He got the little fella dressed, which he was starting to get pretty efficient at…and changing diapers was a bit easier. Thank goodness, because he was horrible at it in the beginning. He still was far from perfect but was encouraged because he was starting to get cute smiles from the little fella. Especially when Zane held his hands and let him stand on his feet and try to walk—not that he was yet ready to walk, but Nicky enjoyed trying.

And he loved that activity walker, with its four

wheels. He could slip Nicky into the seat and the kid would instantly use his feet to push himself around the room. Zane had realized that some things had to be moved to higher ground because the kid had pushed his cart over to the coffee table, laughing as he tried to pick up the heavy bronze horse Zane had sitting there. Zane had enjoyed his antics and moved the bronzed horse. He realized as he carried the horse to the kitchen table that he hadn't laughed in a long time.

He thought about his nephew and that beautiful wife of his, the mother and dad of this cute fella. Emotions swamped him with just the thoughts of what they were missing. He shut down the memories and thought of the positives instead. He had to focus on those and keep his chin up for this baby boy and get him on a positive road to his new life. And going to the grocery store with this little fella was part of that. He'd thought about calling Alice or any of her daughters-in-law or Maggie—she had been so good with Nicky. But no, he had to do this. He had to get used to being this awesome baby's daddy—stand-in dad. Others took their babies to the store, and actually Nicky wasn't a tiny baby; he was soon to be eight months old and showing enthusiasm at getting around. So this was just something he was going to have to get used to, carrying a kid around with him. He was very accustomed to going to the grocery store with being single all his life and being a chef. It was needed and he enjoyed shopping and surely, he could push a cart with a little fella strapped in. He could do this. So he walked out to the truck, loaded Nicky into his car seat behind his seat; then, after securing the door, he climbed in, strapped himself in, and took a deep breath.

"Okay, little fella, you ready?" He looked in the rearview mirror. All he could see since the carrier was positioned facing the seat was the kid's feet moving as if to the sound of music. He chuckled. "Looks like I wasn't the only one ready to get out of the house. Let's do this."

A gargling sound came from the back seat, and he smiled bigger. One day, that kid was going to start talking and that was going to be fun. He remembered how fun it was when Nicky's daddy had started talking. It had been fun to hear his words and fun listening as he'd learned to put words together into sometimes funny combinations.

He pulled out onto the road and headed toward the store. He found a parking space and pulled into it, turned off the engine, and climbed out. Within just a few moments, he had the grinning boy propped on his hip as they headed inside.

"We're going to test this out," he said as he entered the store, headed for the buggies. He was distracted by Nicky grabbing his shirt and popping his head against his shoulder as he reached the buggies; he was looking at the kid. "You are one funny little fella," he said as he reached for the cart's handle and froze as his gaze locked with the startled eyes of Lisa.

"Hi," he said. "I didn't mean to try to steal your cart." He stepped back so she could pull the cart from the others.

"How is he doing?" she asked, her gaze stuck on Nicky.

The baby's gaze was locked onto her, and he grinned bigger than Zane had ever seen.

"He's doing good. Honestly, I've never seen him

smile so huge. He doesn't get upset much, other than the first few days at the hospital when he was missing his…parents. But he's doing good. Obviously, he likes…you."

He had rambled on probably more than he should have, but it was apparent that this little boy liked what he was looking at. And, of course, Zane couldn't dispute it because it was the truth for him too. He'd always remember that day in her office when he first saw her…she was stunning.

"I didn't get to see him awake and had no idea how alert he was. Goodness, he's grinning at me. And his eyes…so green. A better word would be emerald."

"Very good description. He got those from his mother. I remember when they found out they were going to have him, Dave wanted the baby to have Becca's eyes. And his wish came true."

"I'm sure she was beautiful, with eyes like that. Well, I don't want to hold you up, so I'll leave you two to it. Anyway, he's adorable, Zane." She gave him a hesitant smile, then reached out as if to touch Nicky's cheek, and then stopped and pulled her hand back. "I'm sorry, I almost touched him, and I know it's not good to go around touching babies in grocery stores. You know, spreading any germs I might have picked up off my cart or something. Have fun." Then she turned and pushed the cart away from them.

Zane stood there, locked in place, watching her head away from them. Nicky reached out as if to grab her, and he had to hang onto the boy. The kid grumbled; he looked down at him and saw his lips trembling. He swung toward the carts and grabbed one. He moved out of the way for the people who were coming in behind them. Once out of everyone's way, he set Nicky into the seat and attached the seat belt to keep him steady—along with his hand that rested on the boy's shoulder. Once he got him situated, he pulled out his list of products and headed into the main opening of the store. He scanned left toward the fruits and vegetables, and then he scanned to the right, trying to see whether he could spot Lisa. But he didn't see her.

Then he had to ask himself, had he planned to go in her direction if he saw her or head the opposite way? It was a complicated question to answer.

Pushing the cart forward, he kept the hand holding the cart next to the baby's hand that was resting on the front rail; he couldn't be too careful and wanted to make sure he kept Nicky safely in the seat. Even though he'd strapped him into the seat with the cart's baby straps, this was a first for Zane and he had to get used to keeping the baby safe. Then, taking a look at his list, he stuffed it in his shirt pocket and grabbed the cart with both hands. He pushed forward as he tried not to think about Lisa.

That was an avenue he didn't need to go down, and he was tired of being distracted by her. But he had to say he'd seen care, or something, in her eyes that was appealing when she looked from him to this sweet boy. Of course, he could understand it. The love that he'd felt for this baby had grown to where it filled him up. He'd never felt anything like what he felt for Nicky—even the love he felt for Lisa was different. *Why was he going down this path? Stop. Do not go down that path anymore…*

He inhaled sharply but the thoughts kept coming. Feeling love for an adult, he realized, was amazing, wonderful, and for him, had never happened before falling for Lisa and getting himself in this miserable situation. But enough of that. From everything he knew about this child's life, he knew that loving him as much as he did, it would never be as much as Nicky's wonderful dad and amazing mother had loved him. Loving the baby wasn't hard; the amount he felt for the boy made him walk on air.

Heart on a rampage, he pushed the cart in the fruit area and picked up a plastic carton of strawberries and one of blueberries and placed them in the cart. Then he picked up a cluster of green grapes and also a cluster of purple grapes, and looked from one to the other and then at Nicky, who was reaching for both.

"Okay, which kind do you like best?" He lifted one, then the other. Nicky's gaze followed each, and then he laughed and tried again to grab one. Zane laughed. "Looks like we're taking both home." *Looking for grapes had never been so fun*, he thought, as he placed each in a plastic bag and then into the cart. He then found some salad items for himself, tomatoes and bell peppers. He was looking forward to next summer when he'd grow some of his own vegetables in the side yard. Once he had all the salad items, he grabbed some bananas and then headed to the meat section. He rounded the corner and that's when he saw Lisa again. She stood beside an open freezer in the center of that section of the store and she stared down, motionless.

Unable to stop himself, he pushed the baby and cart over and stopped beside her. "Are you buying an already packaged steak for the restaurant?"

She jerked her head up and stared at him, clearly startled, as if she'd been lost in thought that had nothing to do with the packages of steaks.

"N-no. I'm off tonight and was just trying to grab something for me to eat tonight. But at the moment, I can't figure out what that will be. I'm not really hungry."

Her words had him glancing down her figure, suddenly realizing she'd lost weight. She had a full figure—a perfect figure, as far as he was concerned—but today her slacks were looser than he remembered them being. "Are you not eating?"

She crossed her arms and looked from him to the

baby, who was looking up at her with that huge smile on his face again.

His emerald eyes twinkled with…happiness. Zane was shocked again by the baby's reactions to her. It was similar to the way he felt each time he saw her, with her shimmering soft green eyes. "He is really infatuated with you."

"He's so adorable. But I feel bad for him if he's infatuated by me."

"Why?" He was, or had been, infatuated by her.

She brushed her brunette hair behind her left ear. "I just mean there's a lot of other people for the charming little fella to be infatuated by." She smiled at Nicky, and his smile grew; then he gurgled and chuckled, and she chuckled too. "He's adorable and his smile is wonderful. Did his mom or dad have his smile?"

Zane swallowed the lump that instantly formed in his throat and met her kind eyes. "He, um, he has his mama's eyes. That great emerald tone. And he has his daddy's smile. And then he's a combination of everything else. It will be interesting to see him when he's an adult. Hopefully each of his parents will stand out in him but give him his own look. I like that he has his mom's eyes. They were beautiful like she was, and his dad's eyes were always great to see. He—" Zane faltered and looked down, needing to relieve the pressure behind his eyes, not needing to have tears of grief and regret roll down his face.

"I'm so sorry." Lisa reached out and cupped one of his hands gripping the cart.

His eyes automatically met hers, and he saw the sincere sympathy in her beautiful, soft green eyes. "It's still an emotional subject."

"I'm sure it is. I can't even imagine. You know, I don't have a child and I never will at this late date in my life. But I can't imagine having a child and leaving him behind, so young." She squeezed his hand. "But Zane, obviously they knew what they were doing when they left him with you. You are going to be a great daddy— and I know you aren't going to be his true daddy, but he'll grow up with you in his brain and heart as his daddy. And he'll be wonderful because of your guidance."

They stared at each other for a long moment.

"Dada," Nicky exclaimed.

Zane's gaze flew to the baby's excited face.

"Dada," the baby said again, grinning as he looked around the room as if looking for his daddy. Then his eyes grew sad, and he looked from Lisa, who looked stricken, and then his eyes slammed into Zane again.

"I'm sorry," Lisa whispered.

Zane couldn't move as tears began to stream down Nicky's face. Zane reacted, unbuckling the boy and cuddling him in his arms as the sobbing grew louder. "I've got to go," he said, and then he left the cart and headed for the door. All he had were soft words of comfort to whisper in the baby's ear as he snuggled his face in Zane's neck and cried for "Dada" and "Mama."

CHAPTER SEVEN

Lisa hadn't known what to do after watching Zane and the sweet baby leave the supermarket. The expression on little Nicky's face sent an electrifying pain sparking through her. She had almost started crying there in the middle of the meat department, watching them leave. Finally, she'd gotten hold of herself and put Zane's groceries in her buggy, then gone to the checkout line and paid for it all. Then she'd gone out to her car, got her things into one bag and his in a couple of others, and now here she stood at Zane's carport door.

Her heart thundered as she fought the want, the need to cry again for that poor baby. She lifted her hand

and knocked as her heart pounded. She bent down and picked up the bag she'd had to set near her feet, and she waited and hoped and prayed that her being here wouldn't upset Zane.

The door opened and Zane stood there, pain still written on his face. He had loved his nephew and lost him. His nephew's wife had also been special to him, and he'd lost her too. Lisa understood the pain of losing someone. She'd lost the man she'd once loved…the man who'd used her, betrayed her, and the man who— thank goodness—she knew she no longer loved. The man she could no longer even imagine that she had once thought she loved him. She'd gotten over all the pain he'd caused her and was grateful she was over the man. But that kind of emotion wasn't something Zane or this baby had; they had that deep, everlasting love for the couple they'd lost, and her heart ached so very deeply for them.

"I brought your groceries. I knew you would need them, and I also wanted to check on the baby. I hope that's okay. I'll leave if you don't want me here." She held the packages out to him. He swallowed hard and then took the bags from her, his fingers grazing hers as he took them. Warmth flowed through her at the connection.

"Thank you. I…I'm sorry I left like that but I'm still learning to deal with this and the baby and what he's going through. These circumstances are so…" His voice trailed off on the last words.

She gave him a gentle smile. "I understand, and you've handled it well. Is he okay now?"

"Yes, I got him home and distracted. He's in his walker now, there in the living room, chattering to his zebra that I grabbed the night in the store when I was stocking up on things before heading here. Thankfully he likes the little zebra. I think he must be telling the zebra his pain, and since I don't understand the rumble of words he puts out except for the two he spoke at the store—" He looked away, clearly thinking about that moment again. Then he zeroed in on her again. "Yes, please come in." He stepped back, holding the door open with his back as she moved inside into the utility room that led into the kitchen.

She could not mess this up. They had their problems, but this baby took precedence over everything. If Zane needed any kind of help, she was willing to give it. She walked into the kitchen, and he followed her in and set the bags on the counter beside the refrigerator. She could see the baby with his back to them in the living room, which was on the other side of the kitchen bar. He was scooting slowly around in his walker and talking to the huggable zebra in his hand. His words were merely small mutters that only he could understand; what she'd seen was so sad, as was his situation of being left without his parents, but he was adorable.

Her heart thundered.

Oh, how she had wanted a baby like this sweet child. She had been so ridiculous, with letting her ex-husband keep putting off her desire to become a mother. And then he'd had an affair with a younger woman and had a child with her. And here she was, alone, uncertain and, truth be told, scared of opening her heart to another man, or even just adopting a child on her own. And then there was this baby, who had been so loved by his parents and lost them. She looked at Zane. What a great father he was going to make. But getting here in this manner was not the way anyone wanted to become a parent.

"He looks adorable. Zane, I can't imagine what you feel but you are going to be a great father to that boy. And you handled today very well, honestly. You had groceries and you had a hurting baby who needed your attention. Even if I hadn't been there to bring them to you, you could always go again or call me, or one of your other friends, to go for you. I know I'm not the only one in town who calls you a…friend."

He leaned against the counter and crossed his arms as he studied her. "I thought you just called me an employee."

His words stung. That was basically how she'd labeled it on the beach when they'd had their last personal talk, just between the two of them. She'd told him after he'd kissed her that all he could be to her was her assistant chef and no more. She couldn't remember her words exactly but he had summarized it and standing here now, she knew she'd been so stupid. "I deserved that. I didn't mean all of that. True, I wasn't ready for a relationship. Don't know if I ever will be, but you are a friend. And you might not be able to look at me after feeling emotions for me that you claimed, and I'm so, so sorry. I just can't."

He looked away, and she hated it. She wanted to be able to feel more for this wonderful man. But she just couldn't let herself. She completely knew the pain involved when it fell through.

~*~

Zane stared at the woman he loved and now wished he didn't. In all of his life, he'd never fallen in love with any woman except her. But having stood there, looking at her, his heart thundering and aching at the same time, her words penetrated deep. And like this baby, he knew that the pain she had been dealt by her ex-husband's betrayal pierced deep for her, just like Nicky's loss would.

He met her gaze. "I'll look at you as a friend and thank you for what you've done today, and also for bringing lunch yesterday. When they called, when my nephew called—the sound of his broken voice, the pain of the knowledge…he knew when he made the short call that he wasn't going to make it. The trust that he put in me—I will live up to it. I keep having to tell myself that I would live up to his trust, and I will. Today was my step in that direction. I looked at that sweet baby crying for his mom and daddy, and that alone was the only thing I was focused on. As I move forward, that's the way it will be. So, in that regard, I appreciate your offer.

"And I also understand more of where you're coming from. I would appreciate your help in any way you want to give it. That's how I feel about anyone who offers to surround this baby with love and care—people who want to give him a wonderful life as he grows up. And I can tell you that his mom and dad are looking down right now and thanking you and all the other friends who are stepping up to love him. Honestly, I can never have imagined them granting me this…precious opportunity, to be this baby's—I don't know what to call myself. New father? Guardian? It's hard to know. But I know as I go, I'll feel like his father but having him grow up calling me that will make me feel like I'm stealing something from Dave."

"His father knew what he was doing when he called you. He sounds like a wonderful, smart young man. If he's looking down right now, he's proud to have you step up and into that spot. I can tell you, not that I'm a professional or anything, but this baby will automatically call you Daddy. Look at his age—he's going to know that you've done everything for him and he's going to, soon, put all of that name on you." She had said all of that in a near whisper, obviously not wanting to make Nicky upset again.

"And Zane, his parents probably had made that decision before they were killed because you were always there for Dave ever since his father died. And from what I understand, she had no family either and that was one of the things that drew them together. So they were starting their own family. Little did they know that they, too, weren't going to be here on earth with their child. But they knew that you would be, and you were their choice. Again, I believe they knew what they were doing. You are an amazing man, Zane Tyson, and you're going to be an amazing father to that adorable, marvelous little man in there."

Zane watched her tear up and he did, too, looking at her and hearing her words. Unable to stop himself, he stepped forward, wrapped his arms around her and she placed her head on his shoulder as he held her. "Thank you. I'm so glad I chose to move here, across the bay to this small town. I'm always grateful that your ad drew me here. So, yes, please be my friend."

And he knew in his heart that if this was the way he had to take her into his life that he would do it for Nicky and even for himself.

~*~

Her world was spinning, here being held in Zane's arms, and Lisa struggled to stop it. However, she knew this was a good place to be, that from here on out, it was not about her and Zane but it was all about the sweet baby. In that moment, she felt a bump against her legs. She lifted her head from Zane's strong shoulder and looked down into the sparkly eyes and smiling face of Nicky. She smiled spontaneously, her heart filling with love for this precious baby. She stepped back and Zane released her, which was a good thing. She dropped down to her knees so she was face-to-face with Nicky's smiling face.

"Hey, little fella. How are you? I like your little zebra." She reached out and touched the soft black-and-white zebra.

Nicky pushed the stuffed animal toward her. He muttered some undecipherable words, making her smile ever bigger—something she hadn't believed possible. She took the zebra, which made Nicky chuckle, and she heard Zane also, which was a wonderful sound as she kissed the zebra on the head and pushed it back to the boy. He copied her and kissed the zebra on the head and pushed it back to her. She kissed it once more and handed it back to him, and he did it again. And suddenly she realized they had a new game. She wanted to kiss this little fella on the head and hoped one day she could, which gave her a huge hope of happiness in doing that.

"You, little fella, are wonderful."

Zane squatted, with his elbows resting on his knees, and looked from Nicky to her. "Do you have some time to hang around for lunch? You could watch him, rock him while I get his bottle. I'm feeding him food now, too, but if he goes to sleep while you're feeding him the bottle, I'll feed him food when he wakes up. He really likes his bottle, and I haven't quite figured out how to get it all on a schedule. So sometimes the bottle comes first and then I can get the real food ready and then it's available when he's ready."

"Yes, I would gladly do that." She looked at Nicky and held her arms out. Instantly, he reached for her. So quickly he reacted that she almost teared up again. She carefully lifted him from the little seat that held him and enabled him to use his feet to move the buggy around the floor. He snuggled against her and her gaze lifted, meeting Zane's glistening eyes. *Why was Nicky so drawn to her?* She couldn't figure it out, and the look in Zane's eyes told her he recognized the baby's reaction too.

Zane stood and then moved behind her and helped her stand, probably to make sure she didn't stumble as she rose with the baby. She moved toward the living room and went to the rocking chair. She was going to ask him whether he'd already had the chair or was it another thing he'd bought before driving all the way home.

"I'll get the bottle ready and bring it to you."

She sat. "Thank you. I'm going to thoroughly enjoy these moments. This child is precious."

He stared at her from across the bar and nodded. "Yes, he is." Then he turned away and began getting things ready.

Nicky kept his head leaning against her but at the same time had an arm wrapped snuggly around his zebra. He looked up at her. "Na," he said, stumbling over the word as he blinked up at her.

"You are an adorable little fella."

Zane walked into the room and handed her the bottle. She didn't exactly know how to feed a baby; she was a chef and never had a baby around to hold. She took the bottle and shifted the baby into the crook of her arm; she offered him the tip of the nozzle and he took it. His eyes closed as he began to enjoy the formula that Zane had fixed him. Her automatic response was to look up at Zane but he had turned away and walked back into the kitchen.

This was all about the baby.

CHAPTER EIGHT

Alice had been glad when she got to work and found out that Lisa had actually taken an entire day off from work. Her two assistants, ladies who had been with her since she'd opened the restaurant and whom she'd passed over when she'd hired Zane as her assistant chef, had now been raised to the level of assistant chefs. She'd also hired two new sous chefs to take their previous positions. It thrilled Alice that her friend was going to finally start taking more than a few hours a day off. Especially considering she no longer had Zane to back her up.

Alice had backups in her position and had hired them in the beginning, and they were fully trained to fill in for her when she wanted to be off. Like today, she took lunch off, hoping to give the new chefs confidence that she believed in their abilities by not being afraid to leave when Lisa was also gone. She was confident in her front desk workers also; therefore, here she was, driving into her driveway at her and Seth's home. She was going to relax for the next hour or so and let the employees run the inn. As she started to get out of the car, her gaze locked on Lisa's car in Zane's driveway. A smile burst across her face and also through her heart. *This was wonderful—hopefully. As terribly sad as the situation was with this baby losing his precious parents, could it be that Zane and Lisa might find each other through helping him?*

She got out of the car and continued to stand there, looking across the yards, smiling. Finally, she forced herself to head inside and not get caught standing there staring. She could not be caught being a snoopy neighbor, even though—very unlike her—she wanted to sneak down there and peek in a window. She could just see her friend holding that sweet baby. She knew how much it had hurt Lisa, realizing she would never have a child. Alice herself couldn't imagine never having had her boys, and that was the reason her heart had ached so much for her friend. Fifty-four years old was not an age anyone hardly ever had a child. So Lisa knew her chance had passed long before she'd actually divorced her ex. While married, he'd put off her want of having a child; then it had been too late, and then he'd forsaken her with someone else and had a baby with her. And left Lisa as if she were a piece of trash he'd thrown out the window, as though she were worthless. Just the thought infuriated Alice.

She set her purse on the counter, then went to look out the window at the ocean view.

Her life had never been like that. She'd had the pain of losing her first love's love on that horrible day when William had drowned in the river. But then, when the time was right, sweet Seth had entered her life. Oh, how she wanted Lisa to know what love like she'd been blessed twice to know was like. Lisa deserved it.

She had liked Zane from the moment he came into the restaurant and applied for the job of assistant chef. He was a wonderful man, a very talented chef—his food was as amazing as Lisa's. And Alice could tell just by the way that he looked at Lisa that there was something there. Lisa could deny it as much as she wanted but there was no way that Alice would ever believe Lisa didn't have deep feelings for Zane.

She stared out across the beautiful blue water. The water where she had so many wonderful memories, watching the wind blowing over it, carrying her hopes and dreams. All of her life, her hopes and dreams had been carried on this wind surrounding Star Gazer Island and now it carried them all for her sons, their wonderful wives, and hopefully soon-to-be wife Maggie. And now, as she stood there, looking out over that water, she prayed that it would be a new start here for her friend. That the happiness would billow over Lisa and Zane and sweep them into an undeniable romance, interlocking their hearts and their lives. Lisa needed a new start.

~*~

Nina strode across the gravel of the wide ranch parking lot from the gate of the house to the barns. She knew exactly which barn she was heading for and didn't have to call out or search for Jackson. He had come out to check on a couple of colts that had been born a few months back and he kept close to the house. They had a large cattle sale coming up and he and Tucker had been busy getting everything ready. She walked with her hand on her growing tummy. It still had a way to go but it was round now and visible, and she loved touching her tummy. Knowing her baby rested inside there thrilled her. She walked into the stable and headed toward the back, where it opened up into a small pasture.

There he stood, leaning against the opening, watching the two colts romp around in the circular pen. He heard her approaching and glanced over his shoulder, instantly smiling, and held out an arm. "I'm glad you're joining me. You just made my day."

She slid both of her arms around his waist and leaned her belly and baby lightly against his hip. She looked up at him and he looked down at her and smiled, then bent his head and kissed her. Oh, how she lived for these moments.

He took his time, then lifted his head. "Yep, you

just made my day."

"I'm glad I could do that for you since you did it for me. So, are you looking out there and thinking about our baby playing out there with them soon?"

He chuckled. "Well, I can guarantee you he won't be out there running around anytime soon. But I can pretty much bet that in a short few years, we'll have another couple of colts and he or she will probably be out there romping with them. I remember we all were. Me and Tucker and then Dallas and then Riley brought up the end, and we all had to keep that little kid rounded up more than the colts. There was nothing we liked better than getting out there and romping with the colts. Of course, the colts didn't always know we were playing with them and every once in a while, we'd get kicked. But pretty soon we got to be good friends and they all grew up to be well-rounded, good horses."

"And y'all grew up to be really good men. Cowboys. Wonderful guys. Of course, I think you're the very best of all, and I'm blessed to have you as my husband and the soon-to-be-father of my baby."

His smile widened. "We are really having a great

conversation tonight. You are really lifting me up. Is there something you want, or need?"

She chuckled. "I always need you but no, I just came out to spend a little time with you. You've been busy working on the auction with all your paperwork, and I guess I have been neglecting helping you. I'm going to have to make some calls and get the dinner set up."

"If you don't feel like setting up the food, we can hire it done easily. You just let me know. Speaking of that, have you been feeling morning sickness anymore? At the beginning, you seemed to have those days but lately you don't seem to be as bothered."

"I'm better. The morning sickness has slackened this last week, but I get tired and when I do, I just sit down. But no nausea lately, which is awesome. So I'm back there in my office, painting like usual. You can come back there and see my new painting. I just painted a beautiful, morning sunlit pasture scene with a pregnant horse." She paused and smiled. "And another horse and tiny colt. A newborn from the non-pregnant horse. I think it's turning out wonderful. I think it represents your family—well, all of your brothers and wives. I'm pregnant and so is Lorna. Pretty soon, one of us will have a baby and one of us will still be pregnant. So I'm thinking about that in this painting. Lorna's going to have her baby a week or two before me and the horses are like that. It just kind of came to me after I started painting that day. In this picture, the colts are going to be born a little apart, but I think in more pictures I'll show them growing up together, playing and romping…it's just a new idea I got to portray the growing family. In this picture, the horses represent us McIntyre brides as we grow this family…others will include the father horses—yes, I know the right word is sire but to me they're the daddy horse. Same way with me calling a mama horse a mama."

His smile widened. "You call them whatever you want to call them. I love this idea. I can just imagine an entire collection with a growing number of colts running and romping and a bunch of pretty mama horses standing to the side, enjoying the scene. And maybe you'll include us fellas in a few. And then Sophie and Riley too. Hopefully soon. I know she's ready, even though they've not been married long. Riley talks about it a lot. And then Tucker—he's ready to get married but content to give Maggie the time she needs to say yes. But I can tell you if they don't have babies right off the bat like us and Dallas and Lorna, they are going to be great uncles and aunts. And they'll *also* make great horses for your pictures." He grinned and leaned in and kissed her cheek.

Nina shivered with delight at the feel of his lips and his enthusiasm for her painting idea. "And your mom and Seth are going to be amazing grandparents, so I'll have to figure out if they'll be humans in a painting or older horses. I love them so much. This conversation has me thinking of our baby and all the people who are going to love him or her. Like Lisa. They're going to know her as an aunt, I believe."

"I agree."

Her thoughts went to Lisa. Oh, how she wanted that wonderful woman she'd met when she'd met Alice as they'd started the inn there beside her home—where Lisa now lived—to find love. "I want Lisa to find happiness so much, Jackson. She deserves it. And your mom was telling about Zane coming home with the baby his nephew left to him upon his death. Such a sad story. I'm sure they had friends who would have been good parents, but they chose Zane, even though I think he's in his early fifties. And they chose him. I think it's wonderful."

"I agree again. That hits hard, too. We're going to have to think about this. What if something were to happen to you and me? Who would we choose to raise our baby?"

His words slammed into Nina, and suddenly she felt dizzy. She sucked in a breath. "Oh, Jackson, I don't even like thinking about it. Yes, naming someone the guardian of our child is something we haven't talked about. Something I can't stand thinking about, even though there are so many wonderful people in our family who can step up to that spot. I want to be here to see our child grow up."

He cupped her face between his hands. "Shh. You will. It's not something I wanted to think about either. Even knowing we are blessed with a great group, it's us who we want to raise our child. But it is something I now know we need to talk about." He leaned in and kissed her forehead.

She realized that he was right. "There are so many wonderful people to choose from. What will we do?"

Jackson shifted his back to the wall, and drew her to him and studied her. "That's a good question. Everyone is wonderful and capable but still not us. But we need to do this. I would instantly say Mom because she did a good job with all of us, and she's going to be involved with the raising of our sweet baby. However, she's older and just married and we can't put that on her shoulders. Maybe we need to talk to everyone about it. They are all going to have to make similar choices. Just looking at what Zane is going through is eye-opening.

"So, I'll be asking my brothers that question. Asking them if they would want to take on something like that, or if they have a reason they wouldn't feel right about it. Or if they think one of their brothers would be better. I can tell you one thing: if something were to happen to me, and you were left to raise our child alone, I know you would have the complete help and support of all of them. If something were to happen to both of us, whoever agreed to do this would also have their support. Gee, I was out here thinking pleasant thoughts and now I've got this in my brain. It's the most important choice we can ever make."

She reached up and cupped his cheeks as the emotion in his voice and eyes matched what she knew hers to be. "It is so very important. But we also have the relief of knowing that we have a vast, wonderful group of family to pick from. Not everyone is so blessed and they have to choose from friends and pray they have a friend who would step up. It's a huge responsibility and must be taken seriously. So, we are blessed in that matter. And you know, it makes me think that after we have this baby, we'll have to add more to the list of babies they'd be willing to raise." She smiled as his lips lifted and he chuckled.

"Yes, we aren't going to look at this as if we're going to give birth to this wonderful baby and then it'll be over with. We're going to keep building a great family and think positive about it and be happy because I can tell you, darlin', I love you dearly and I could have babies with you all the time. Every one of them will carry a part of you in them, and it will make my love for you grow and grow."

She lifted up on her toes and planted a kiss on his lips. He embraced her and picked her—and the baby—up off the ground and kissed her. Oh, how she loved this man. Loved his family, and was so happy she'd turned up in this town and met his mom and then met him. Sometimes what you think is a horrible thing—like the stalker who she'd come here to hide from—turns into a good thing. Being here in hiding had changed her life. And suddenly she knew that if something did happen to her or Jackson, her baby would be here, surrounded by wonderful, loving people.

CHAPTER NINE

"**S**o you went over to Zane's and helped him with the baby yesterday?"

Lisa looked up from the paperwork she was working on and wondered why in the world she'd revealed that to Alice. She knew Alice wanted her and Zane to get together as a couple. It was very clear what her friend wanted. She hadn't meant to lead her friend on by telling her about yesterday. She didn't want to lead herself on either. She had thought about yesterday all night long.

Thought about that sweet, wonderful baby and the feel of him in her arms. "Yes, but…it wasn't as if he invited me over. I went to the grocery store and he went to the grocery store, and we met at the grocery carts. We said hello and then I moved on and gave him time to get the baby in the buggy. Then I was in the meat department when he came there and we started talking about the baby. And well, to be honest, it was my fault. I asked him about the baby's mother and daddy. And instantly the precious boy brightened up and began scanning the store as if his mom and daddy were coming down the aisle for him. After a few seconds, his expression turned to pain and he started crying. It was heartbreaking. Zane also looked distraught and he took the baby out of the cart and hugged him to his chest. My heart was breaking in that moment, looking at them and hearing the crying baby and knowing how much he wanted his parents. Zane glanced at me and then left all of his food in the buggy and headed down the aisle and, I knew, out of the store.

"I watched them go, feeling so upset for both of them, and then I looked down at the cart of supplies. I felt horrible, so I got the groceries into my cart, went to the checkout and bought them, and then I took them to Zane's home. I carried the bags to the side door and knocked. I knew he could turn me away but I still needed to deliver the food I had caused him to have to leave behind. I really didn't know how he would react, but I ended up being invited in and I was able to help him with that sweet boy. Thank goodness he had gotten over his crying and gotten distracted by his adorable stuffed zebra while he pushed himself around in his walker around the living room. Zane asked me if I would feed him his bottle while he fixed lunch and some sweet potatoes he could mash up for the baby. I said yes. I couldn't pass up that opportunity, so I did."

She thought of holding that precious baby and watching him suck in that bottle with his little eyes closed and his fingertips gently popping up and down on that bottle as if he played a piano. And then he went to sleep in her arms as he finished the formula. It was like nothing she had ever experienced in her life. When she looked up, Zane was watching, a mix of expressions on his face. It was a combination of sadness and wistfulness in his eyes. She could just imagine that he was wishing she'd never shown up.

"You were a blessing to him in that moment," Alice said. "And you act like you love him."

She gave her friend a point-blank look. "It's a sweet, darling baby who has lost everything, and then here I am, a woman who never had any of that. A woman who wanted it with all her heart. It just makes me feel bad, but I looked at that precious baby who has lost his parents and I so loved holding him. It makes me feel guilty. It made me feel lost. When I got home yesterday afternoon, I walked the beach." She sighed. "And, Alice, I cried my heart out for what I'd lost and what the sweet baby boy lost. And then there is Zane. I don't know what to say about him."

Oh, she knew, but it was getting harder and harder to deny that she loved him. Just the thought of admitting that terrified her. She wasn't one to believe she could be longed for or obviously kept around. The idea that she could expose her heart, admitting her love, froze her up. To believe that that amazing man—that good-looking, strong, wonderful man—could believe that he was really in love with her was something she couldn't do. She knew that he would one day find someone perfect for him…and in her heart, she knew that when he did and she and he were married, that he wouldn't do to her what her ex had done by having an affair behind her back and a baby. No, Zane might realize one day that she wasn't the woman of his dreams, but he would never leave her behind or have an affair. He would just forever wish he hadn't married her, hadn't thought he loved her and not waited for the woman he was meant for.

She rubbed her forehead. She knew that just didn't seem like Zane. He was not like her ex, who'd never regretted at all what he'd done to her. She couldn't compare Zane to that creep. She couldn't compare such a wonderful man like Zane to that piece of trash.

"Lisa. Lisa," Alice leaned forward in her seat across the desk, "let go of what that skunk of a man did to you. He was the loser and the idiot. And you can't let him mess up the rest of your life. Believe me. You know me—I was blessed with two wonderful men who loved me. But because I knew love first from William, I could have let that, the opposite of what you have, stop me from accepting that I had fallen for Seth. Then I would have missed out on this wonderful life of love I'm living now. I was blessed twice. So, see, it could have gone both ways—I could have been doing what you are doing, although for you it was a horrible first marriage, and you let that keep you from having a wonderful life. And—I just need to point something out to you—to be a blessing to that good man and that sweet baby. Don't you even realize what you could be for them? You could be so helpful. And I'm just going to say it out loud—he loves you. He can't even hide it. He *loves* you."

Her heart thundered. She wanted to get up and storm out onto the beach and slam herself into the sand, sit there and let the ocean wind blow some sense into her. But in that moment, she didn't even think she could stand up, she was so unnerved and disturbed. Her friend, who was trying to help her, stood and came around the edge of the desk, leaned down and hugged her.

"Don't let that thing from your past mess up your future. I'm going to leave you now. I know you're going to need some time alone, and I'm not going to pressure you." She pulled back and looked Lisa in the eyes with eyes of her own that said how much she loved and cared for her.

Alice had helped her so much to get through the betrayal and rejection she'd felt and was just trying to help her. "Thank you, Alice. It's just not something I can promise."

"I know. I'm just putting it out there in the open. In real words. And letting you know what I think and hope you'll do."

And then she watched her friend walk out the door, pulling it closed behind her in case she needed time alone in her little office. She was relieved that she had her two young chefs to help take up the slack and give her moments of relief. She needed some relief right now. She longed to hold that baby again.

And no matter how much she tried not to think about it, she longed to feel Zane's lips on hers like she had that night they were on the beach together. This was not where her mind needed to go but that was exactly where it had gone.

~*~

Maggie had finished her book, the romance novel that she had begun when she'd come to the McIntyre Ranch with only trying to start over on her mind. Tucker's sweet sister-in-law Nina, who'd been her and Mark's friend, encouraged her to come out here to the coast where she now lived, and so she'd come. When she'd agreed to come, she was determined to put her life on a new road, to a new beginning that she knew Mark would be rooting her on to do. And that included her writing, which she loved, and that was what Nina knew would help her get her thoughts back in order.

Tucker had been a total and complete surprise. Not at all something she would have expected or even thought of. But, as she now stood on the dock of her home, she thought of the trip that she and Tucker had taken to pick up the things she wanted to bring here before she sold her home and then to have the other things packed and stored until she had her new life decided on. Tucker had been wonderful and now in her home, she had a few pictures of her and Mark, and she loved looking at them. And she had her tall, unique blown vase of many colors sitting on the end of the bar next to the wall. It was four feet tall and a twisted array of colors of the rainbow. It was a beautiful work of art. Looking at the vase had always made her smile. It reminded her of love: the different colors and shades of love, the excitement of love, the tenderness of love, the soft, gentle emotion of love. The bond of those bright and soft tones all blended and intertwined together had done only one thing since she'd placed it on the counter in her new home: reminded her that love would always be with her, that love could blend together in her heart.

She stood there on the pier. Well, it wasn't really a pier; it was the long length of concrete that ran along the yard between the grass and the ocean, making room for a boat if she ever wanted one. There was also a ladder down into the water in case she might want to swim or she happened to fall in and needed an easy way out. She'd placed a couple of chairs at the end with a small table and a metal lounge chair for two that rocked with the push of a foot. It was a perfect place to sit with someone she loved and watch the sun set. *Someone she loved...* It was time.

She could feel her sweet Mark's hands on her shoulders as he turned her toward the house. *It's time.* His gentle words filled her ears, and she walked up the path and to the car. It was time—not a time of sadness but one of happiness and determination.

She turned on the ignition and backed out. Part of this decision had come from yesterday when Zane had called and asked whether she would like to come and watch his sweet baby for a little while. She had pretty much raced over there, filled with joy. She'd taken that baby into her arms and they had had a wonderful few hours while Zane let himself go do whatever it was he needed to do. When he came home, she had had the time of her life. And she had wanted so much to fulfill her dream of babies.

Yes, spending time with Nicky had been all she'd needed to know the direction of her life. She'd come home and forced herself to stay home all night just to make sure what she was about to do was exactly what she wanted. And this morning, she had sprung out of bed, hurried to the shower, washed her hair and her body, pulled on her clothes, put on just a little bit of makeup, and she'd come out here to breathe some fresh air and say a quick prayer and to talk to Mark.

And he'd been there. She could feel his arm across her shoulders as he urged her to do what she knew was right, and that was to give in to her heart and the love she felt for Tucker. She was smiling now as she drove through town and over the bridge, then headed down the road toward McIntyre Ranch. Her thoughts whirled. There was a sense of relief in knowing that she was making the right decision. The one that was right for her. Her heart hammered as she drove up the drive to the ranch. She knew they were planning a big sale for next weekend and that meant he had to check all records and make sure all the cattle were ready. His brother Jackson would make sure all the other paperwork was ready, so both of them were more than likely in their offices instead of off on the ranch somewhere. She pulled into the barn area and up to the stables, where she knew his office was just inside the large opening.

Jackson was walking out of the building as she got out of her car. He stopped and smiled at her. "Hello there. It's nice to have a visitor. Are you doing okay?"

She smiled at him, trying not to let herself go ecstatic with joy. That was for Tucker. "I'm great. I'm looking for your brother."

Jackson's grin spread quickly across his face; then

he nodded toward the stable. "He's in there. I just left him. He'll be glad to see you."

A soft laugh escaped her. "I'll be glad to see him too. And it's been nice seeing you also."

He chuckled. "I get the hint. I'll head back to my office and leave you two to have a good visit."

He was still smiling as he walked away, and she had a feeling he knew something had shifted for her. It was probably written all over her face. It was written all over her heart. She strode through the entrance, took four steps and then, without knocking, she opened the door and walked inside. Tucker's desk was in the middle of the room, with his file cabinets behind his desk and a couple of chairs between where she stood and where his desk sat. He looked up and his eyes widened when he saw her. Oh, that amazing smile. She watched it spread across his face and she couldn't move. She had to fight off tears—tears of happiness, not sorrow.

"I wasn't expecting the day to get this good but I can tell you I'm overjoyed to see you standing there." He stood and, as if sensing something important was happening, he strode around the edge of the desk and then stopped. "Are you okay?"

"Yes…" She fought the tears off again. "I'm wonderful." And then she bolted forward. His arms opened wide and she threw herself into them. He wrapped her in a tight hug, lifting her off the floor as he clutched her tightly so their lips met. They kissed deeply, and the emotions inside her and between them surged as she let her love for him shine in the kiss. Then she pulled her head back. Tears streamed down her face. "I love you. And these are tears of happiness, because if you still want to marry me, I am so ready to say yes."

His smile was so full of love. "I am ready. So very ready." Then he lowered his wonderful lips back to hers and spun them around as he kissed her, as if this were the beginning of their life together.

And she hung on tight and kissed him back the same way.

CHAPTER TEN

Tucker was flying high, holding the love of his life and knowing that now they were going to plan a wedding and a future together. He kissed her as he always did, with every ounce of his love, but he could feel more in her kiss to him now. She'd crossed over into fully loving him, and he was so thankful and humbled at the same time. *What had happened?*

He drew his lips away, finally needing to ask. "I'm raging full of joy about this. But did something happen to bring you to make me so happy?"

Her sweet smile spread across her beautiful face. "You were so wonderful when we went and picked up my things before the packers carried the rest of it to storage. It was reassuring to know that you really understand my everlasting love for Mark, and it eased my mind. I knew I loved you with all my heart, and I always will, just like I felt for Mark. My heart is full and ready and wanting to share the rest of my life with you. But then, yesterday, when I went to watch Zane's baby for him, everything came together. I want to have a family with you, Tucker McIntyre. I want to raise a family with you, and I'm ready. Absolutely nothing is holding me back." She smiled. "I even felt Mark pushing me toward the car to head out here and tell you this."

His heart filled his chest as he took her words in. "You are the same way about Darla, so I totally understand. We're meant to be together, Maggie. Now, when are we getting married?" He grinned, knowing she was going to tell him a date later in the year, but at least they'd have a date.

"I'd say tomorrow but that's not long enough to get a license. I loved Sophie and Riley's wedding on the beach, with your family there and the gentle sound of the water. But we fell in love on the ranch, so can we have the wedding there? I'd love for my close friends from Plano to see where I met you, where my return to living life again began."

"You really want to get married soon? And yes, the ranch will be perfect. Wherever you want it will be perfect, as far as I care. As long as I get you, I'm good with anything." He was grinning and completely in disbelief that his world had turned this beautiful. "Are you serious?" He was overjoyed and still spinning.

"Yes, I really do. And I want it small, here on the ranch, so do you think we can head over to the ranch house and tell Nina and Jackson our news and get them to help us plan a small wedding with just family and then a gathering for our family and friends afterward? Though I want to include Zane and the baby as family since they unknowingly helped me realize I wanted to move forward in my life. And Lisa, too, because she's so close to your mom and seems to be struggling to move forward in her own life. I personally don't know all of her story, but at dinner the other night it was written all over her that there is something going on in her head that has to do with Zane and that sweet baby." She smiled so very thoughtfully. "Like you and I in our beginning, being situated close with the cabins so near each other helped us. Maybe coming to our wedding will help put them in each other's vicinity."

She was matchmaking and he liked it so much that he almost laughed out loud with enthusiasm. "I'm all in. Darlin', let's take a walk. Nina and Jackson are going to be excited about everything coming out of your delightful mouth. And my mom, she's going to be ecstatic. And with her and Lisa, we won't have to worry about something to eat, which will also have Lisa committing to come no matter how much she might not want to be around Zane and the baby. Then again, we might be wrong, and she might be looking for reasons to be around them. Anyway, everyone is going to be thrilled because they've been waiting and rooting for us to get married. So, come on, let's go over to the house and get this celebration started. Wait—what about your mother and Archie?"

"I'll let them know and hopefully they can be here. But if not, since they are on a lifetime adventure, then we are doing it anyway—with their blessing, I can assure you. Those two have probably been praying for this to happen." She lifted up on her tiptoes and kissed him again, a quick but still very nice kiss. Then she took his hand and spun out of his arms, and they headed toward the door.

When they walked from the stables into the morning sunlight, they were startled because near the house were Riley's and Dallas's trucks. And they all stood on the back patio. "I think this could be an accident but I'm not positive. We'll soon see." He smiled at Maggie.

She was already holding his hand; now she clasped his bicep with her other hand and leaned close. "This will be exciting."

As they walked through the gate and down the walkway to the patio, they all watched them. It was easy to see in all of their expressions that there was a hope that he had good news. He loved his brothers. He really did. They had stood with him through his heartache and through the years of struggling through the sorrow, given him his space and now they were just standing there, holding back excitement. They clearly were hoping he was going to tell them what they wanted to hear.

He and Maggie stopped at the edge of the patio, and he grinned beyond control as he looked at them. He held up his and Maggie's united hands. "We are getting married."

Cheers went up instantly and then they were swarmed by his enthusiastic family members. His brothers grabbed him in hugs and Maggie too; laughs and excitement swirled around them.

"We are glad you're joining the married club." Riley clapped him on the back.

Emotions and the thrill of it all rumbled inside Tucker as he smiled at Maggie, who was being swept into Nina's embrace. "I'm so happy to be here. Happy indeed, brothers."

Nina squeezed Maggie with great enthusiasm. "I knew it," she said. "Lorna and Sophie are going to be so excited, too, and hate that they aren't here enjoying this wonderful moment we're all experiencing."

"I'm sorry they aren't here either, but we are going

to let everyone know. But the guys are going to have to tell their wives because we have to tell Alice next." Maggie leaned back as Nina eased her hug up. "But we wanted to see if y'all wanted to help us put together a wedding here on the ranch. This is where we met. You brought us together, without even realizing it. So we want to have a small wedding with family and a few friends. I'd like to have it today but I know it takes a few days. But can you and the guys, if they want to help, and Lorna and Sophie help get it together? I really want to marry him as soon as possible."

She smiled at the dashing, wonderful smile that her words pulled from Tucker. Oh, how wonderful it felt to make him happy. And it was easy to tell that making her happy thrilled him. That was something else he had in common with Mark. It was not something to ignore, and she could not wait until she could give this wonderful man a baby. Just the idea as she looked into his eyes sent a shiver of delight through her. Just looking at the darling baby last night as he snuggled in her arms had set her straight.

"We will be thrilled to do this! Are we talking about

three days? This weekend? Oh, next weekend we have a huge cattle sale, so this place is going to be packed, so that wouldn't work. If you really want to do it in a hurry, we can make sure Alice and Seth can come and we can have a great wedding out here this weekend. Sophie and Lorna are going to be so excited. I can't wait to see their faces when they get to embrace you in person like I just got to do. And Alice will be all in for anything. She'll be so overjoyed, she'll cancel anything that might stand in her way to be here. So anyway, I'm rambling because I'm so excited and oh goodness, my excitement has gotten my baby to moving in my tummy. Oh, he just kicked the wind out of me, goodness gracious." She chuckled hard and her hand cupped her belly.

With a huge smile, Maggie placed her palm beside Nina's on her belly and she instantly felt a kick. "Oh, my goodness, she kicked you—I mean, don't know if it's a he or she but if it's a she, she's going to be one strong little gal. If it's a little fella, he's going to be strong too. Wow. I love it."

"I do too. I can take anything this little baby wants to give me. It lets me know he or she is healthy. And he's as excited about your wedding as I am. So all right, y'all." Nina looked around at the guys, and Maggie did too. Every one of them had a grin on their face as they'd been watching their discussion. "So, are y'all all in on getting these two lovebirds married? And how about this weekend, if everyone can make it?"

Tucker laughed. "You two just tell me when, and I'll be here."

"And that's why I love you. Let's do it. Thank you, Nina. You have fulfilled all of my hopes of getting married to this man quickly."

Nina hugged her again. "Oh girl, believe me, I'm as thrilled as I can be. I've just wanted to get you back to the wonderful, happy person you were before when I knew you. This is perfect, so let's get this wedding going."

Zane had just finished giving Nicky his morning bath and dressed him. The adorable little boy had sat in the kitchen sink, with Zane's hand on his back so he could make sure the kid wouldn't reach for something and throw himself out of the sink. The kid was active and could crawl really good. One morning, when he'd sat him on the floor then turned his back to get the television remote, Nicky had crawled all the way down the hall and was disappearing into his room when Zane turned back around. He was reaching for a tractor out of the box when Zane reached the room. It was as if he liked to crawl better than being in his four-wheel walker he roamed around in when Zane was working in the kitchen.

"So you want to play with the tractor?" he asked as he walked into the room when his phone rang. Instantly, Nicky turned toward him and grinned at the ringing noise. His grin made Zane chuckle…which was something this baby was good at doing. Zane let Nicky grin as he pulled the phone from his jeans and saw that it was Tucker. "Good morning, Tucker. Good to hear from you. How's everything going?"

"I've got some news for you," Tucker said, and Zane could hear excitement in the younger man's voice. "But first, how are you doing?"

"Me and this little fella are making it better every day. I'm adapting and it's a big help that he likes my fresh food that I churn up for him to eat. He also likes baths in the sink like he just had, and now he's grinning at me while I talk to you. So all is surprisingly good here. Now, what is it you wanted to tell me?"

"Well, me and Maggie are getting married this weekend, here on the ranch. And we want y'all to come. Maggie specified that she wants you and that adorable baby, as she calls him, to come."

The news was amazing. "I am so happy for you. I know you've been waiting to hear it. And sure, Nicky and I would love to come. But are you sure? I mean, I can't guarantee he won't decide to start chattering or crying for some unknown reason. Are you having a family wedding? I mean, I'm completely excited for you both but we aren't family."

Tucker chuckled over the phone line. "You might not be family but I'm going to tell you, buddy, that you and that baby that your dear nephew and wife left you to raise helped me and Maggie move forward. When you asked her to come watch him and she did, with great enthusiasm, you have to know it made a difference. Holding him and playing with him opened her heart up to her future and what she wanted. She knew it was time to stop mourning, to stop holding back and to move forward. She came to me the next morning and told me she was ready to get married and to have babies." The smile in Tucker's voice was brilliant, even over the phone.

"That's wonderful," he said.

"We are so in debt to you. I am so thankful to that sweet baby. I was going to hang in there as long as it took for Maggie to decide whether she could remarry… Oh, I know she loved me; there was no doubt about that. It's just she's already lost someone she loved; I did too, so I completely understand. The thoughts that held her back were the same that held me back for so long—what if I lose someone again? It's tough, but when she first saw the little baby, I knew something hit her. Watching the baby for you helped her realize she really wants to have children, just like I do. And one of her big specifications was that you and Nicky come to the wedding, so please say yes."

He was grinning. He couldn't help it. Just the thought that this little baby could help her understand her emotions and feelings meant a lot. Zane's eyes grew moist just thinking about his nephew Dave and sweet Becca, his beautiful wife. He missed them so much, but this was a wonderful piece of news that at least helped deal with the grief. There was no denying that little Nicky was a huge blessing. "You just tell us when, and we'll be there."

"Great. I'll let you know the time but it's this Saturday. We're having a huge sale on the ranch the following Saturday, so that put that off and Maggie didn't want to wait any longer, so when Nina said, let's do it this coming Saturday, we were all in. Maggie would have married me yesterday if we'd have been able to get the license early. But anyway, it's coming up at the end of the week. We told Mom this morning, and she's outrageously delighted. And just so you know, Lisa is also invited. We look at her as family too, so I wanted to let you know. I don't know exactly what's going on between y'all right now but thought it best to let you know she'll be there."

"Thanks. I can't really completely figure it out either. We're working through her path too. She turned me away but came over and brought my groceries after we ran into each other at the grocery store. The baby started crying after she asked about his…well, I can't say it or he'll start crying again. But she asked about the two most important people he lost in his life and she called them by the names any child would call his parents, and he instantly recognized what she was saying and began looking around the store with a huge, excited smile. He beamed and was expecting to see them. Then, when he didn't, his face fell and he burst into tears. I immediately took him into my arms and then walked out of the store, leaving my groceries behind. All I had on my mind was getting him somewhere I could comfort him."

"I'm so sorry. Did it work?"

"Yes, and Lisa felt so bad that she showed up at the house with my groceries and an apology. Nicky had calmed down and we talked, then she rocked him to sleep. I honestly don't know where we stand now, but me and this cute baby will be at the wedding."

"That's wonderful. And, Zane, I have to tell you, she's been through a hard time by being so deceived and so, buddy, you just hang in there."

They said goodbye and Zane let Tucker's words sink in as he looked at Nicky. *Could he hang in there? Should he, when he had so much on his heart that had to do with bringing this little boy up? Did he have extra heart to reach out and try to continue a relationship that could be rejected again?*

He took the baby outside. He needed some space, so they went down to the pier and he stood there, looking out over the blue water. The moment Nicky saw the water, he started scrambling to try to get out of his arms and to the water. He was holding the baby securely but his sudden reaction to get to the water had Zane throwing his other arm around him too. Even then, the boy was still reaching for the water. It was beautiful, with the calm waves reaching up out of the water gently and the sun shimmering on it. The baby laughed as the soft wind blew in his face and threw his head back. Zane chuckled, too; the sight was so adorable.

"I think you like the ocean. You'd like the beach,

too, I think." *Had this little fella ever crawled on the sand? Felt the ocean water on his feet?* Just the idea suddenly had Zane wanting to go to the beach. To get out of the house for a little while. To do more than being stuck in the house. There was more out there, especially here on Star Gazer Island. He just had no beach. He only had a grassy lawn that led to the boat pier, and then you could fall right in that water. That reminded him that he had to get the fence up, separating the dock from the yard. But right now, he had other things on his mind. And as he turned and headed back toward the house with a babbling child who was now trying to reach over his shoulders toward the water, he knew this was going to be a fun day. He was going to make certain of it.

CHAPTER ELEVEN

L isa walked down the beach, enjoying the wind blowing her hair from her shoulders. Enjoying the freedom of having her hair down and not hidden underneath her netting. It was a beautiful day, and she was determined to keep her spirits up. She'd been so excited for Tucker and Maggie, when Maggie had called and told her they were getting married and that they really wanted her at the wedding. Also, if she wanted to come up with a light, easy-to-do wedding buffet for the small family gathering, then they would let her. But only if it was light and easy.

She smiled, thinking about it. Just the idea of them limiting her so that she wouldn't overdo it and enjoy the wedding fully touched her. Maggie and Tucker were a sweet couple, and she was so excited for them. And so was Alice. She'd come into the office with a huge smile of delight on her face. She'd waited until after the call before coming in, having obviously known when her soon-to-be daughter-in-law was going to give her the official invite.

Alice had been so happy, and her words echoed in Lisa's thoughts. "I'm so excited that they are going to finally get married. They remind me so much of me and Seth. Both of us dealt with our grief and our newfound love, and so have they. It makes my heart almost burst. And they really want you at the wedding. You are family, and this is a family wedding."

Maggie had also told her that Zane and Nicky would also be there, that she had requested them to be there since the little boy had meant so much to helping her realize what she wanted. But she didn't want that to keep Lisa from coming if there was a problem between her and Zane. All of them being there was important to her. Those words reached in and touched Lisa. Here she was, at Star Gazer Inn, surrounded by all these sweet people, this family who she had begun to think of as family in the center of her heart, and they wanted her there. They were thinking of her as family also. It touched her heart deeply. She told Maggie and then Alice that she would be at the wedding. Yes, they were her family now, and she was going to celebrate with them.

She had also understood why they'd invited Zane and the sweet baby. Zane had come into this town and made it his home. He'd moved in a few houses down from Alice and Seth, and he and Seth had become friends. It was as if she had her close friend and now her close friend's husband considered Zane as his close friend, and if she and Zane were a couple, it would be perfect. They could all spend time together at dinner or out on a boat ride. Instead of having her dear friends have to be worried about inviting them both to the wonderful celebration because they were worried neither of them would show up because the other one might be there.

She stopped on the beach and turned back to look at where the inn was visible far down the beach line. Her small red house on the other side of the inn was a tiny red dot, she was so far away. The exercise had been good for her. Today was her day to get her exercise and hopefully get her brain resituated after following Zane and the baby home with his groceries and then rocking that baby. Her heart, just thinking about those moments, pounded now, like someone pounding on a door to get in and change her mind and thoughts from what she'd been letting direct her movements.

She turned toward the water. It was a beautiful, calm day with gentle, soft waves flowing in and a breeze that made the shining sunlight pleasant, and it swept over her. She watched a fishing boat riding by, out past the swimming area that had plenty of swimmers out, enjoying the day. Children's laughter drifted along on the air and made her heart long like it had so long ago to hear her own child laughing on the beach as they had a great day. She wrapped her arms around herself and tried to fight off the sadness that came with that thought. Her having a child would never happen. Every once in a while, someone in their fifties would have a baby, but she knew her time was gone. It was a dream she would never have.

Her thoughts instantly shifted to sweet, darling little Nicky cuddling in her arms as he finished his bottle and then slept in her arms as if he belonged there. *Just like it would have been if she'd had her own child.* Sighing, she let the breeze blow over her, float over her tight skin, and tried to make her face relax from the grimace of her teeth and the aching of her heart, thinking of that precious baby and how he affected her. Wishing she was holding him again with his little heart beating against her heart. She opened her eyes, not even having realized she'd closed them. *What was wrong with her?* She turned around; it was time to go home.

The sandy beach in front of her was nowhere near like the more crowded area now behind her. There was a section that was pretty blank, other than the back of a tall man in emerald-green swim trunks and a white T-shirt that showed off broad shoulders and muscled arms. All that was topped off with soft brown hair, slightly wavy and playing around on his neck in the breeze. She froze as the hair reminded her, as did the physique, of Zane. Her heart thundered as her gaze was drawn from the man to what he was turned toward and watching.

Just a few feet from him, on the ocean's edge, the soft, small waves washed in and dispersed to a thin roll of water sliding up the shoreline, brushing slightly at the knees and hands of the tiny boy crawling in the water toward a tall bird that stood on the sand. He had left his yellow sand bucket near what she now clearly knew were Zane's feet as he headed toward the bird. It wasn't dangerous, she could tell; just a joy to see the expression as the baby looked over his shoulder at Zane with a huge grin on his little face. He laughed, then looked back at the bird and started a fast track for the bird. She chuckled at the same time Zane started across the short distance to make sure the long-billed bird didn't turn toward Nicky and cause a problem. She was frozen as she watched the scene in front of her. And then, as Zane reached the water and the big bird did turn back and look at him, she smiled. Then, automatically, she pulled her phone from her pocket, opened the photo screen and snapped the shot: the baby and the bird, and off to the edge stood Zane, the protector.

Her heart clinched tightly with longing as she slid the phone back into her pocket, and she strode slowly toward the perfect picture of happiness.

Zane chuckled as he watched Nicky trying to reach the tall bird that stood with his feet in the water like Nicky, who had his hands and feet in the water. The bird was very tall, with his long legs coming up from the water to his feathered body. It stood there, as still as could be, not seeming to realize that he had totally captured the baby's attention behind him. The bird stared out at the water; obviously something there had his attention, probably a fish.

Nicky crawled through the water but not real fast, but with his full attention on the bird. If Zane had felt any danger, he would have closed the few feet between them if he needed to but there was enough distance between the boy and the bird. The bird was not interested in the boy sneaking up behind him; he was concentrating on the object that only he could see in the water. It was kind of funny, because the bird was watching something in the water, the baby was watching the bird, and he was watching the baby.

The baby had gotten close enough that he expected

the bird to look over his shoulders, so Zane strode the few feet forward and scooped Nicky into his arms. Wet dripped between them and he smiled as they both watched the bird look at them before he took off, sailing low over the water and then lifting up into the sky with the ease of a leaf caught on the wind and being swept easily up and away. Behind him, he heard a soft noise, and he turned around. His heart jumped as he realized there had been one more in the leg of watching the bird, as there stood Lisa, and she'd been watching him, the baby, and the bird. She was smiling—she was beautiful.

"So wonderful. I loved watching that sweet boy be so infatuated with that awesome bird. I hope I haven't interrupted. I was walking back toward the inn and came up on y'all."

He realized he hadn't said anything as she spoke the last words quickly, as if trying to hurry and get on her walk again. Maybe trying not to interrupt his and Nicky's beach time. Nicky swung his arm out, and Zane looked down to realize that the baby was, as usual, studying Lisa like he studied no one else. He waved his arms toward her, clearly making it obvious that he wanted her to hold him. "Well, it looks like you are now drawing his attention rather than the bird."

She smiled as her gaze went from him to Nicky. She took a step closer. "Can I hold him? Do you mind?"

"He's wet. He's been crawling around in that shallow water a bit."

"I don't mind." She reached out, and Nicky practically threw himself into her arms as she scooped him out of Zane's.

Zane stood, transfixed. *What about her drew Nicky like this?* Of course, he knew why he was drawn to her, but that wouldn't be why the baby wanted so badly to be in her arms. The baby had seen others; he'd been drawn to Maggie also, but not like this.

She looked up and caught him studying her. "Is something wrong?"

He blinked, realizing that he must have really been staring hard. His thoughts had taken over. "No, not at all. I am just trying to figure out..." He paused. *Would his words sound weird?* "Okay, so don't take this wrong, there is nothing that I mean by it, but he reacts differently to you than he does to anyone else. I mean, he really likes Maggie. She kept him the other night, and he liked her from the moment he saw her. But he acts completely different when you walk up. Look at the way he's looking at you. He's snuggled in your arms…he's looking up at you as if—" Zane's thoughts slammed to a halt. He suddenly realized what it was.

Lisa was fifty-three or four. She seemed younger than him, but she was actually a few years older than him. But she didn't seem like it, didn't act like it; she was just wonderful. He'd never really thought about the age difference; he just liked her. But this baby was picking up on something and in those moments, it suddenly hit him. Lisa's dark brunette hair, with the soft auburn highlights, the green eyes, and the smile…suddenly he understood. She reminded this child of his mother.

Stunned that it took him this long to realize the similarities, he was more stunned by how Nicky took to her. Obviously, the baby knew she wasn't his mother…wouldn't he? *Sure he would.*

"Zane, you're starting to worry me. Why do you look so alarmed?"

He blinked at her words and turned away to stare out at the ocean, letting the breeze flow across his face and hopefully ease the muscles.

"Sweetie, you are adorable," Lisa cooed as she suddenly stood in the water in front of him. She'd left her sandals in the sand and now she walked a little deeper to where the water rolled over her ankles.

Zane's gaze drifted down Lisa in her soft yellow top and her white shorts that hit just a few inches above her knees. He yanked his gaze back up to her pretty hair. Hair that had shifted across her cheek as she bent slightly forward and pointed at the small bit of wave swirling about her ankles.

"Do you want to walk in the water?" she asked, smiling at Nicky, whose face he couldn't see at the angle he was standing.

But he saw the baby squirm, as if wanting his feet in the water like hers. She lifted him from her hip and, holding his hands, she placed his feet in the water between hers. And they began to walk down the beach at a slow pace. Nicky chuckled loudly, then jumped so that she was holding his hands and his feet came out of the water; then both landed into the water and created a splash. Both Nicky and Lisa instantly laughed as water sprayed up into his face and some even reached her face because she was leaning over as she walked with him in front of her.

Zane joined them in a laugh and then strode so that he was beside them as they walked. She slid a pretty gaze his way and seemed to reach inside him with her intense stare. "What?" he asked quietly.

"Why did you look so alarmed a few minutes ago?"

He rubbed his temple. "He is drawn to you not just because he likes you, but you remind him of his mother." He didn't say the last word out loud but clearly formed it with his lips.

Her expression went to a look of shock; then her brows met, and her lips trembled.

"Don't get alarmed. Obviously, it's not something that bothers him. He likes it. I think he knows the difference, but he's drawn to you." And so was he, but for totally different reasons.

"Splash me again," she said, pushing lightness into her voice as she smiled down at Nicky when he leaned his head back and grinned up at her.

She lifted him from the water so he could kick at

the small waves with his feet and squeal with delight. She chuckled and placed him back in the water while holding him in a standing position so that he could kick and squat down to his heart's content. She looked over at Zane. "So she had dark hair like mine? Is that what makes us similar?"

"Her hair was brown, with some of those highlights like yours. It was thick and all one length and hit right below her shoulders. So very similar to yours, but that wasn't the only thing. She had eyes that were an emerald tone, slightly different from your sparkling lighter green, but it's just the overall effect of your coloring, your eyes, but mostly your smile. You and Becca both smile similar, and every time you are near this boy, you smile…and it makes him smile. I have to believe he's thinking about his mother when he's looking at you." He realized he'd said mother out loud but had realized the baby would know mama but not the bigger word.

Tears sprang into Lisa's beautiful eyes. One flowed over the edge of her eye and rolled down her cheek. He wanted more than anything to reach out and gently wipe away that tear but he kept his hands to his side.

"I know it's a bit of a hard thing to know that. But

even though I think he's drawn to you because of that, I think there is more. He's drawn to you because you're so nice with him. He likes it; he's at ease with you. And you shouldn't just think he likes you because of the resemblance. There's something more. So don't just think that's the only reason he lights up when he sees you."

She rubbed her cheek on her shoulder, getting rid of the dampness. "I wish she hadn't died. I wish he hadn't died. This sweet baby deserves them, deserves the goodness they would have been giving him. But I still stand by my previous words—he's very blessed to have you in his life."

"I realized quickly that I'm very blessed that they thought of me and had me on the papers to be the one to raise him. I can raise him with many memories of his parents. I can keep him close to them in that way."

"But you can be there for him, and he will love you like you are his father." She whispered that word, but Zane was certain the boy had no idea what *father* meant yet.

He stopped walking and so did she. They stared at each other, and she gave him a gentle smile, her pretty lips lifting up at a slight angle on the right side. His lips lifted, watching.

"I need to go back and get my sandals." She lifted Nicky up and spun around to place them facing in the opposite direction. When she spun, it must have been the water and the wet sand beneath her feet because she wobbled and was about to topple to the side in the deeper water with her hands holding Nicky's so he, too, would have gone down.

In a reflex, Zane stepped forward and swept her against him, watching to make sure her hands were still holding his precious laughing boy. The feel of her against him and the sound of Nicky's laugh had him smiling as she looked into his eyes with her beautiful ones. Heart pounding like twenty pro basketball players racing for the net, he wanted so much to kiss her but his new parenting mindset kicked in. He steadied her, then eased away from the softness of her body. "Glad I could save you from a swim."

"I-I'm glad you were able, too. Now, this cute little fella might not say the same thing." She laughed as she looked down and he did, too, to see Nicky bending down to crouch in the small incoming wave that gently hit him in the chest. He responded with a loud, boisterous laugh that had him and Lisa joining in their gazes, locking with happiness that this baby brought both of them.

But in that instant, Zane knew for him it was more than that, and there was no way of denying it or pulling back from it: he still loved this wonderful woman with all his heart. He'd never, ever in all his life loved anyone else. Never been drawn to anyone like he was drawn to Lisa from the moment he entered her office for the interview to be her assistant chef. Never in his life had he wanted anything more than he wanted her in his life. Wanted her to help him raise this precious baby who he loved with all his heart and wanted more than anything in the world to do right in honor of Dave and Becca.

But he knew the timing had to be right, and right now, he just needed to let Lisa enjoy her moments with Nicky. Maybe he was being weird, but if she fell in love with little Nicky, then maybe she would let herself admit she was in love with him.

CHAPTER TWELVE

"I'm so excited my wonderful Tucker, who suffered such loss, is getting married," Alice said as she and Lisa entered her office in the back of the inn. She sat down on the small couch with the recipe books she'd carried from the kitchen and smiled at Lisa as she sat down too. "We all watched him in these last seven years getting over his broken heart and now we're preparing for his marriage. Wonderful Maggie came into his life and now we have another happy beginning."

Lisa reached out, placed her hand over her dear friend's hand, and squeezed gently. "I'm so excited for them. We've watched and we've all known they were in love; the time just had to be right. Thank you for inviting me to be a part of the family. It really means so much.

Now, we have to come up with a great tasting, easy meal as requested by the sweet bride." She smiled, remembering Maggie's words.

Alice turned her hand over and held Lisa's tightly as she grinned. "I see you got the picture, and we can do it together. You can cook anything from hard to easy. And their goal is that we all come together, have an easy and happy gathering, and no one overwork. Visiting and having a great time is their goal."

"It sounds great, and yes, we're going to do this together." Lisa smiled, loving this friend and partner so much.

"So, are you going to be okay being there with Zane and Nicky being there?"

Lisa had been expecting that question. She patted their clasped hands with her other one and then let go, stood and walked over to the window as her thoughts rolled over her answer. She studied the patio and the people enjoying their stay here at the inn. She took a breath and turned to face Alice. "I am. I didn't tell you, but he and I ran into each other on the beach and it was so fun." Emotion came into her voice, and she had to calm it down. She did not need to get emotional. She had done so last night just thinking about walking on the beach with him and that precious baby. And that bird. Oh goodness, that big bird just added to the picture. It was just a fun thought, how the baby wanted to chase that long-legged bird. She wanted, not the big bird but the big picture, and she knew it. "Alice, when you let go of what you'd had and opened your heart to what was in front of you with Seth—I'm asking a question that I believe I know the answer to but I need to ask…have you ever regretted it?"

Alice stood and walked over to her, and placed a hand on each of Lisa's arms. "No, I haven't, and I never will. I didn't let myself give in to what my heart knew was right. Not at first. But I didn't shut the door on it, and sweet Seth, he had patience and he waited. He gave me emotional support and showed me his love through that support and patience. So what are you thinking?"

Lisa swallowed hard. "Well, I closed the door. Actually, I slammed the door on what Zane offered me. He…before the horrible accident happened, he had met me on the beach one night. Well, I was on the beach, making a decision, and he unexpectedly showed up. I was trying to tell him that nothing could ever be between us when I paused in exactly the wrong moment before telling him that. I know now that I paused because my heart was telling me not to say those words. When I paused, he kissed me. I'll never forget that kiss. It was so very wonderful. I mean, I've never felt what I felt in those moments. But I couldn't, so when it was over, I finished what I had been trying to say, that as far as we were concerned, we were simply working in the restaurant together. That I was simply the chef and he was my assistant, and that I could never have a relationship. He took what I said and left. Then we made it through the next couple of weeks, him simply working and not speaking much, just there getting through a shift. He didn't look at me much, only did what he was required to do, and I could tell he was deciding when he should quit. Then he got that call from that sweet, precious baby's daddy. I have not been able to stop thinking about it. Then seeing him with Nicky—Alice, I messed up."

Alice instantly embraced her. Lisa let her tears roll

down her cheeks. She had so messed up. She had let her horrible first marriage experience take control of her life—steal her future, a future that could be wonderful. But there was the baby and the fact that Zane was younger than her. By a little over three years. He could find a younger woman. He could find a woman several years younger than him and make absolutely certain that the baby had someone there closer to the baby's mother's age. At least closer than she was to Becca's age. When Lisa let go of Alice, she told her exactly that.

Alice held her gaze and didn't blink. "Lisa, I'm going to tell you right now something heartfelt and serious. Do not talk yourself out of this. Don't shut him out. Just move forward. Don't rush it—I know that scares you but let it happen. Let's plan this wedding's food and have a good time doing it. And then let's see what happens, but remember that Zane may be feeling more cautious since he has the baby now. So he needs some time. I don't know, I'm just saying that we've all been through these hard times, that sometimes—as you well know—time is what we need. So just smile, be open, and let's see where this goes."

Lisa loved this woman. "Yes, I am so happy to have you by my side. Let's do this. Let's get this wonderful meal decided on. We'll get it done that morning and I'll bring it out there and we will celebrate. And I will wait and watch what happens in my life but that day, this week even, is all about Maggie and Tucker's new start."

~*~

Zane had a good couple of days. His mind had been overwhelmed with thoughts of Lisa and determination that he would fight to win her over. He wouldn't just walk away—do as she'd asked and go on any longer as if he didn't love her. Because he did. He loved her with everything in him.

He glanced over at Seth. He and Seth and Nicky were on their way out to the ranch to meet with Tucker, Jackson, Riley, and Dallas to figure out where and what Tucker and Maggie wanted to do at the wedding, leading up to them saying their vows and afterward.

His mind was filled with thoughts of what he would do at his wedding with Lisa. That was the only wedding he was planning, and he prayed it came through for him. If she held out and turned him down, he knew there would never be anyone else in his life. He was fifty-one years old, and she was the first person and only person he'd ever wanted to marry. Or ever would want to marry.

He looked over at Seth, who was driving. "So, this is a great day, right?"

Seth met his gaze. "I can tell you, ever since I married Alice, every day is a great day. How's it going with you in making those great days come through?" He grinned, then focused on the road again.

Zane could see that Seth had been waiting to start this conversation. "Well, to be honest, it wasn't going so great. Lisa had pretty much told me we were just friends, so I went along with her but it didn't feel right. I had fought hard to have the career I had in the restaurant industry, making a name for myself, but I realized I was missing out and needed a change. Then I saw the ad for an assistant chef and I looked across the bay toward Star Gazer Island and decided to apply.

"The moment I walked in for my interview in

Lisa's office…Seth, it was like a lightning strike. The minute we started talking, I knew what I wanted, and it was no longer just the job. I wanted her in my life. She hired me, and I bought my house and took building a friendship first and hoping for a relationship. I didn't let my over-excitement about how I felt about her take me too fast. Then when I thought it was time and no denying there was something big and important between us…she shut the door. I was trying to deal with it, trying to figure out what my next step was over the next two weeks. I knew I wasn't going to continue working with her if there was nothing that would grow between us. I was working every day wishing she was my wife and working only as a coworker and knew that couldn't go on. And then I got the call from Dave right before he died." He paused, heart hammering.

He turned and looked into the back seat at Nicky, who was playing with his stuffed zebra while strapped into his car seat. "And then, this wonderful, adorable little boy entered my life. He brought my focus to what is right for him. I've been rethinking everything, thinking I need to hang on while giving her space. You were patient because you lost your first love sooner than Alice, right?"

Seth glanced at him. "Yes, I gave her the room she needed to find her way—and prayed it was to me."

"And that's what I'm going to do. I can't deny it—she's the only woman I'll ever love and I'll wait if I have to. But I'm also not going to just sit on the side and think that I've lost my feelings for her. That would be a lie. So, here's the deal. We're going to plan this wedding, have a good time watching Tucker and Maggie say I do, and I'm going to have a good time myself. And…" He paused, unsure how to say the next words.

"And you're going to romance her." Seth shot him a grin.

Zane let out a chuckle as a big smile flew across his face. "Yeah, that's the perfect way to describe it. I'm going to try with all of my heart to change her mind. And honestly, as sad and horrible as little Nicky's story goes, I can feel my nephew urging me on. When I see the way Nicky reacts to Lisa, I know even more that she's the one. And I know that his parents know it too. If they can't be in his life, I just feel like they are trying to make a way to bring the right ones into his life."

"You have a great plan, and I can tell you that his parents picked you because they knew you would do right by their sweet baby. I can also tell you that we are crazy about Lisa. She's a wonderful person who's had a horrible turn of events in her life, and we are all rooting for her to have a happy ending. You have a whole bunch of folks cheering for this to happen."

Zane smiled, reached over, and put a hand on his friend's shoulder and squeezed hard. "Thank you. Star Gazer Island is the place where I'm determined my dreams are going to come true."

~*~

Wednesday at noon, Maggie walked into Star Gazer Inn. She loved this place and the people who ran it. It was lovely, and everyone was so friendly and welcoming. She was here to meet with Lisa and Alice to talk about the food they were serving at the wedding on Saturday. She had told them to make it easy, that she didn't want it if it had them working that day instead of having a good time. She had a feeling that Lisa should be there and that she shouldn't be distracted by preparing food. But she also knew if she hadn't asked Lisa to do the cooking, it would have hurt her feelings, so she'd settled on simple. And today, as they told her what they'd decided on, she would see whether they'd embraced her wishes.

Lisa was a great chef and Maggie knew her nature would be to do something fantastic and that it would distract her. In her heart, Maggie felt like this weekend was going to be very wonderful, not just for her and her love of Tucker but in other ways also. And those other ways meant Lisa and Zane and that sweet, adorable baby boy who had changed her life in such a wonderful and positive way. She stood there for a moment, just thinking of that baby's tragedy that had brought him to this wonderful island. She prayed for his parents, and she felt them—felt their sadness of not being there with him—but felt that they were cheering on what everyone in her soon-to-be family were also cheering on…and that was Lisa and Zane admitting their love and becoming the parents of that precious baby.

She shook her thoughts and overpowering emotions that just thinking of that brought to her. She also thought of the wonderful positive of it all, that little Nicky had helped her embrace how much she loved Tucker. Helped her walk away from the love of her past and embrace a future with Tucker and the thought of the family they would give birth to together. No, she wasn't going to get to do it with her first love, Mark, and Tucker wasn't going to get to do it with Darla. They both lost those first loves and had been brought together to fall in love, embrace that love and start again. God had put Tucker into her life and she wasn't going to fight it off any longer. And she wasn't going to ignore what she felt like was an important moment in that sweet baby's life either—having the right people in his new life raising him.

"Maggie, I'm so glad you're here."

Maggie spun around and saw a smiling Alice coming out of the hallway, her arms opened wide, and then she was instantly embraced by the small, wonderful woman. Her soon-to-be-mother-in-law. Maggie hugged her back tightly. "I'm so glad to be here."

Alice leaned back, still holding onto her upper arms. "I'm thrilled to have you here. I'm so excited about this weekend."

Maggie was, too; she couldn't help it. The joy was rolling from Alice, and she felt the same way. "I'm excited to be here, and I know whatever you two have come up with is going to be wonderful. I'm anxious to see Lisa. She's a wonderful person. And I'm excited for the menu too."

Alice linked them together, sliding her elbow around Maggie's, and headed them toward the restaurant's entrance door. "She is an amazing friend and chef, and excited to help out and to come to the ceremony. I told her we couldn't go overboard, and she did as you asked. I think you'll love it."

She reached for the door and opened it so Alice could go through first. And she did, but did not unlink their arms as she pulled her to the small registration desk.

A pretty young woman looked up from the computer as they walked through the door leading into the kitchen. It was busy as everyone worked on preparing vegetables and other dishes. There were two ladies about her age discussing something; then they looked up and smiled. They looked as if they were in charge, and she figured the two were assistant chefs, who taken the spot Zane left, and were enabling Lisa to have some more time off. Which gave her space to fall in love—Maggie hoped so, especially for little Nicky's sake.

Lisa came to her office door and drew everyone's attention from them to herself. She smiled at them and waved them into her room. But Alice released her arm, enabling Maggie to embrace Lisa.

"Thank you for doing this, and I'm excited to see you at the wedding."

Lisa hugged her tightly. "I'm looking forward to it. I would have enjoyed your wedding no matter what, but now I'll actually get to sit there and relax. So please y'all come in."

She waited for them to enter her office and then, as she and Alice took the two chairs in front of her desk, she heard Lisa say, "Okay everyone, thank you for giving me time for this meeting. Thank you for what you're doing with lunch today. I know it's going to be great." Then she entered the room and closed the door.

"I'm so excited to see how wonderfully the kitchen staff has come together to support you," Alice said.

Lisa didn't go behind the desk to sit in her chair. Instead, she leaned her backside on the desk and placed her palms on its edge, her fingers dangling on each side of her. She looked completely relaxed as she smiled. "To be honest, it took me a little while to get used to it but I'm adjusting well. They are great, and I'm enjoying more time off. It helps knowing they can handle it. And Alice, like me, they all love working here. Your inn is just wonderful."

Alice glowed with happiness. "I think so, too, and all of you help make it that way."

Maggie grinned at them. "I agree with both of you. I'm not involved in the kitchen but I love the food and the atmosphere. I love the look of this wonderful inn and the gardens and the beach. It's truly a winner and a memory maker. I think you two have done a wonderful job. And the girls—well, you know, your daughters-in-law—they love it too. This is one of the first places they brought me and helped me know that there was life outside of where I had lived. I enjoyed my life in Plano, but I love this small town, this area. The ocean and the ranch are amazing and both have helped me start my life over. So anyway, I could go on and on. You can tell I'm excited and ready for the next chapter in my life. Now, for this wonderful family event, what are we eating?" She couldn't not smile as the two older ladies looked at each other.

Lisa placed her hands together as if she were about to pray. "We are having wonderful enchilada casseroles, which I love. They are easy and delicious, just like you've asked for, and then an array of cheese dips, guacamole, and then a few extra things that taste great and go along with this. If and only if you like this idea. We have more ideas."

"I can just tell you that Lisa knows what she's doing with this option," Alice added.

Maggie smiled. "I love the idea. I can't wait to try them. Why don't you sell them here?"

"It's more seafood and steaks and great lunch options. But I love this and often do it for myself when

I have time. So, are you sure?"

"I'm sure. I'm so happy that I moved here. All of you are wonderful." She almost said something about how much she loved Nicky and what spending that short time with the sweet baby had meant to her, but she held back. She was going to keep this to herself; right now, she wanted Lisa just to have it in her mind that she was supplying dinner for the wedding and that this was all about her and Tucker's wedding. Maggie wanted her there, and prayed that Lisa and Zane would share something at the wedding that they couldn't deny, and that baby Nicky would be the great beneficiary of it. She smiled, thinking that maybe her and Tucker's wedding could lead the way to Zane and Lisa's.

Of course, this was what she hoped, but most of all she was so thankful for Tucker and so very happy they were getting married and starting their new life together. Her heart warmed with love just thinking about him.

CHAPTER THIRTEEN

The tent was set up, and the chairs were settled beneath it. Zane watched the smiling Tucker, soon-to-be wedded man, as he helped with as much as they let him. His brothers, his stepfather, and Zane were all striving to keep him from overworking. They wanted him to be full of energy tomorrow night so that he and Maggie would have a wonderful time at the wedding, at the wedding reception, where they could hopefully dance the night away, celebrating with everyone, and then later with each other. Zane's thoughts on that went to Lisa, despite trying not to.

Earlier, when they'd driven up the ranch's long drive and pulled to a halt, Lorna and Sophie had been crossing from the large tent between the house and the barns. Huge smiles burst to their pretty faces as they hurried to the truck. He got out and opened the back door of the truck and then lifted Nicky from his car seat while they oohed and aahed. When he turned from the truck, holding the baby, their smiles at Nicky instantly put thoughts of Lisa's sweet smile at Nicky into the forefront of his mind.

"It's cute little Nicky," Lorna exclaimed.

"And we're taking him with us, if you'll give us the honor," Sophie said with a playful look, as if begging.

He chuckled and so did Nicky. "Here you go. Take good care of him, and I'll get to work with the big guys."

He and Seth watched then as the baby was whisked from his arms by Sophie, cuddled close as she and a smiling Lorna headed toward the beautiful stone home across the drive. Nicky was giggling at the happy women as they headed inside the house.

The little fella was getting better and better every day, and even though Zane's heart hurt for his parents, he could feel them rooting on their baby's adjustment to his new life.

"Looks like Nicky's going to have a good afternoon

with the ladies. He's adjusting well, it looks like. That was a big, happy grin."

"Yep, it was. He's adjusting quicker than I expected. And yes, about to have a fun afternoon. They are going to treat him well."

"Real well. Alice couldn't wait to see him when I told her y'all were going to ride out with me. You're a good man, Zane. Dave and Becca were wise to name you as the one to love and raise their baby in case anything happened to them."

"I'm the blessed one in this, and the heartbroken one at the same time. But all of your family have been so helpful."

"We want to be here for you and that baby. You know, we're expecting a grandbaby from Jackson and Nina in December. Nicky will be a bit older, but I have a feeling our little babies will be good friends."

Zane paused at Seth's words, reality setting in once again in another aspect. "*Our little babies…*wow. Seth, I have to get used to thinking of Nicky as my child." Emotion gripped him. He was already thinking of Nicky as his, but was that right? He met Seth's understanding gaze, and he cleared his throat. "They'll grow up together and that reassures me that he will have a wonderful network of people around him. His mom and dad knew that, too, from all the things I said about this community after I moved here."

It was true, as he thought about it. Dave had told him in their last true call that they couldn't wait to come down and see him and the new town he loved. *He loved...* It was true: Star Gazer Island was the place he loved. Warmth filled him and a jolt of strength raced through him. "I'll be glad to have you and your great family by my side as we raise these boys—wait, do you know yet what Jackson and Nina are going to have?"

Seth grinned. "Jackson told me this morning that they just found out they're having a boy. So, these two boys can grow up riding horses together...or cooking something good together or building something like tree houses—got to get my specialty in there to rub off on them, too."

Zane grinned. "Hey, I'll take you up on that. All of us can team up on our kids, and they'll grow up knowing how to do everything. I really like the idea of Nicky learning to ride a horse—not that I know how—but it sounds great, like something a boy would enjoy."

Seth leaned his head to the side and dug his eyes into Zane. "If you ever want to learn to ride a horse, you know the fellas will get you on one and teach you, well, like they did me. You'll have a great time. I had never ridden much but Tucker got me on a horse and now Alice and I go riding sometimes. It's great. This ranch has plenty of horses and amazingly beautiful places to see. I can tell you there is almost nothing more fun than riding across that land on horseback…of course, I have to say that riding out there with the woman you love makes it all the more great. Like taking a boat out on the ocean to watch the sunset on the water, watching it set across the land beside the one you love is two of my favorite times in life."

Zane met Seth's gaze that now flashed with questions. "I'm not sure that would be the best place for me, not until I learn how, but you do make it sound great and intriguing." He grinned. "Of course, cooking supper for someone you love is great too." He stood there, staring out across that stunning land with Lisa's face being illuminated by the love in his heart. He loved her, and he was going to have to win her over.

"Anything I can help you with?" Seth placed a hand on his shoulder. "You know, love can be complicated. I thought Alice and I had a lot to get through, and then watching all her sons and what they've gone through, I know hard spots can be overcome. From what I see, and I may be stepping out of line, but I'm pretty sure you and Lisa have been struggling to get the feelings that you share with each other handled or figured out."

"Is it that obvious that I feel what I feel for Lisa? And that I'm struggling?"

"It's obvious. All of us know because you either light up at the mention of her name or looked troubled. All the ladies in the family have noticed and want you two to find your way. Alice says that even though Lisa is a little older than her sons' wives that they all see what she sees in both your eyes when you look at each other or say something about the other—love."

Zane couldn't move. "I love her, but the ball is in her hands, not mine."

And it was…unless he could find a way to help her

see that he would never be like the man she'd once given her heart to. The man who had then tossed her beautiful heart and love to the mud as if she and her heart were worthless. What an idiot that dude was.

Zane would prove to her that he wasn't an idiot. Somehow, someway, he would win her and they'd stand before their friends and say vows of love and commitment.

~*~

At six o'clock that evening, after having determined what she and her wonderful staff would be cooking for the wedding tomorrow, here she was now, arriving at the ranch for the rehearsal dinner. She hadn't wanted to come but couldn't not come after sweet Maggie had invited her. The men of the family were cooking barbeque, so she was simply a guest. She had nothing to do but relax, according to Alice.

Alice should know that right now, the last thing she would be doing was relaxing. She knew that Zane and baby Nicky would also be here, and her heart would be in turmoil. Mixed with longing and need to hold—not just that sweet baby, but that amazing, handsome, make-her-want-him-with-a-simple-look man. She was in trouble.

Taking a deep breath, she opened the door of her Jaguar, stepped out, and saw the large tent that Alice had said would be used for the wedding reception tonight, the wedding tomorrow and party afterward, and then next weekend it would be used for the large cattle sale. It wasn't Alice, her friend had pointed out, but her sons who were making their father so proud; they'd worked so hard to keep the ranch going and growing. They'd embraced what he loved and were making it into what he'd always dreamed it could be for them. Just the thought of how happy and pleased Alice was about the way her life had turned out—despite the tragic loss of her first love and then the finding of her second love—it was so very touching that Alice had had the heart to love one man so much and then be able to open her heart again to a love that was obviously just as strong and deep and now, living a new happy life. And about to soon have a houseful of grandkids, finally.

Lisa's stomach rolled. She placed a hand on the top of the low-slung car to steady herself. Oh, how she envied her friend. She loved Alice with all of her heart and she was so happy for her, but oh how she wished she'd herself know at least that kind of love once. She closed her eyes as reality slammed into her. Practically slapped her. Because she knew she'd turned down the opportunity to know what Alice had been blessed to know twice in her life among her sorrow and loss. Lisa, heart-slamming, heart-hurting female that she was, had closed that door.

She was a chicken.

Yes, plain and simple, she was a chicken.

She sucked in another deep breath, gathered up her floundering emotions, and took her first step toward the tent. Music floated about. She was a little late, because it had taken a lot of convincing to get in that car to head out here. She pulled her shoulders back and put on the face of happiness that she'd done many, many times when she'd hosted all those business dinners for her creepy ex-husband. Hosted them all before she'd found exactly how he'd been using her to build his business with her great cooking, pleasing smile, and hosting abilities. While he'd been out having a different life with a different woman, who then gave birth to a baby that he'd denied giving to Lisa all those years as she'd aged to a point she could no longer have a child. A baby she'd so longed to have for years.

At least the music was happy and as she pushed herself to join in on the happiness that she felt for sweet Maggie and wonderful Tucker, she found she was walking faster and steadier, determined to enjoy their happiness despite her unhappiness.

As she walked through the opening, she watched all the things going on. It was a huge tent and this small, basically family, gathering was not going to take all the space that would be filled with tables next weekend for the cattle buyers and horse buyers who would be coming. Tonight, there were two sections set up. On the right was a beautiful arch full of roses and greenery. There were two small rows of chairs for people to sit in and watch vows being exchanged. There were freshly cut flowers and a lot of beautiful greenery set up and it was wonderful. Then, to the left, she saw the tables set up and the men, the McIntyre brothers, as they talked and prepared the meat for the pits that were outside the tent opening behind them.

She looked over at the other table, where the women were gathered behind the table of drinks and desserts. And then there were the dining tables with white tablecloths with clear vases full of pretty sunflowers and red roses. It was going to be a beautiful, though not aggressively over-decorated wedding. It was simple and uniquely joyful. She could see that in all the smiles of everyone. Among the men, she saw Tucker, the groom, had a smile that radiated. Despite the trials and heartache of losing his first love, he'd been able to find what his mother had found: new love for an aching heart. Her gaze shifted over to the ladies. They smiled and talked to beautiful Maggie, the bride, who'd also been through heartache and the loss of her first love. Here, on this amazing ranch, she found love again.

Everyone standing there, not just Tucker and Maggie, had been through trials and tribulations and were now happy again with new love and the excitement of new babies who would be coming in December.

Lorna held her adorable toddler, who was grinning and trying to get down to roam but his mother held onto him. In Alice's arms was sweet Nicky. Her heart clinched just seeing the smiling baby. He looked up at her friend and lifted his little hand and touched the edge of Alice's jaw. Oh, how she was jealous of her friend in that moment.

She then heard a familiar voice from the other direction. Her gaze automatically shifted to the sound and she saw Zane enter through the opening from the barbeque pit, carrying a large tray of steaks.

"Where do you want them?" he asked.

The man was such a wonderful chef. He'd quit working for her but here he was, helping prepare something special for this special night, and she knew it was going to be delicious. She stood there, not having taken a step or turned away, but instead just stared. He stopped walking and his gaze locked onto hers. She saw longing there in his gaze that was quickly replaced with no emotion. It hurt seeing it come and go so quickly, but she deserved it. She'd told him there was nothing between them. But with this baby, they'd shared some lovely moments. Undeniable moments, yet they were denying them. He was because she had basically demanded it.

She looked away, feeling horrible. She closed her eyes. *This was not about her. This was not about Zane.* This was about Tucker and Maggie, and she hadn't put that into it before. Opening her eyes and inhaling again, she stepped toward the women just as Alice spied her, grinned happily, and called her name as she jiggled Nicky on her hip and waved her over. There was nothing in that second that would make her frown. That baby lit up and his arms flew open wide as he grunted something she didn't understand, but it was sweet nonetheless. She headed straight to him; she smiled at Alice, who instantly handed him over. All the women were watching her, and she knew that they could tell how she felt because there was nothing about this sweet, darling baby she could hide. He held her heart.

~*~

"Are you okay?" Jackson asked, drawing Zane's gaze

from where he was watching Lisa cuddle Nicky as if she cherished him with all her heart.

Zane looked into his friend's eyes. "Yeah…actually, I don't know what I am. I'm a little lost at the moment. My heart comes up with one answer to my problem, then turns away from it, trying to do what she's asked of me…then I see her with that baby, and my heart aches for everything she tells me she doesn't want." He looked back across the room to the beautiful smile on her face as she looked at the baby with eyes Zane couldn't see because of her angle. But he knew they were full of love for Nicky.

Jackson took the tray of meat from him. "Go over there and see her."

Zane took a deep breath, his brain rolling over what he needed to do. "Look, Jackson, I thank you for what you're trying to do but I think right now what I need is some time outside to get my brain back right."

"Then go on. You got this great meat done, so you just take your time. But, Zane, think about not just what you need but what she needs, and the baby. If you think y'all need each other, then I'm going to urge you not to back down. I needed Nina. And Nina needed me. Maggie could have probably gone on and made it with the love of her first husband deep in her heart. And I know that Tucker could have done it, too, with the love of Darla in his heart. But Tucker watched all of us, including Mom, fall in love. His heart healed, and it was the perfect timing for Maggie to enter his life. I want you to think about that because from what I understand, Lisa has an injured heart and maybe you stepping in is what she needs. She just hasn't quite come to grips with it yet."

His smile reached in Zane's heart, like an awakening fist. "You don't look like a guy who would back down from someone in need, or someone you love. That's what I see in you. Plus, you really can cook extremely well, and so can she. Anyway, go outside. I just needed to let you know that we are all rooting for the two of you. We can all look at the two of you and know you're the best thing for each other and for that sweet little boy she is cuddling so very wonderfully right now."

Zane's gaze was locked on her just as she lifted her

gaze and met his. His heart flared, with gigantic heartbeats slamming against his ribs. Their gazes held strong, locked, but hers suddenly flickered with…what? *What was in her eyes? Was it worry? Need? What was it?*

Unable to stop himself from walking over there and asking her that exact question, he turned and walked out of the tent. And he didn't stop walking until he was at the stables. There were several colts in the pens. He locked his elbows on the second rod of the arena, his back bent and weight on his arms as he leaned forward and rested his forehead on his crossed arms and stared down at the ground. Emotions tried to overwhelm him, so he inhaled deeply. He didn't need to let the wrong emotions overtake him. He needed to get the right thoughts in his brain. Needed to think of what was best for everyone.

CHAPTER FOURTEEN

"**O**kay, everyone," Alice said, beaming brightly as all the gals turned to look at her.

This included Lisa, whose insides were twisted from the penetrating look in Zane's eyes as he'd studied her from across the room. She looked down at the baby, concentrating on his happiness as he toyed with her necklace and chattered happily. She adored looking at him and tried hard to concentrate on him rather than the expression, the look of longing in Zane's eyes.

"We're going to go over to the wedding area," Alice continued. "And we're going to take our seats. Well, some of us are taking our seats. Lisa, you and that darling baby boy are sitting beside me and my baby, Landon," she said as Lorna came over with Landon and he reached out with his arms for her. "I think he was jealous while I was holding Nicky."

Lorna grinned. "I think you're right."

Alice took her precious boy and kissed his cheek as she embraced him. "He has nothing to be jealous about. I love Nicky, and I love this little fella. And I can't wait for his new baby sister or brother to get here. I can't wait for the whole household of babies I'm going to have in the new year."

"And believe me, they will all be thrilled to have you as a grandmother." Nina came up, put an arm around Alice, and grinned.

Lorna smiled. "Yes, you're going to be a grandmother from heaven. I'm so glad I moved here and was blessed to become a part of this wonderful family. And you, Lisa, are part of this family, if you haven't figured that out. We are so glad you came tonight to join in on the family affair."

Lisa's heart hammered. She loved this family. "I'm so glad to be here, because I do feel like a part of the family. I love you all. And I know that Zane, though I can't speak for him, I know he is going to be thrilled to have all of you involved in this baby's life."

Sophie came over, smiling. "And you're going to be in that loveable baby's life too. We can all tell that he adores you so much—just like someone else does." She lifted an eyebrow, meeting Lisa's startled gaze.

Lisa hadn't really talked to any of the others about what she felt for…fought against feeling for Zane, but now she realized that everyone must know as they all looked at her with encouraging smiles. "I don't know what to say to that. I want all of y'all to be happy, and I'm so very glad that Alice is happy. But I just haven't been able to…well—you know, cross that line again after having given my heart so fully and deeply to my ex-husband and to get thrown under the bus." The words rang on the wrong tempo from her mouth. They didn't quite sound right to her. She looked down at the smiling baby and thought again of that look she'd seen in Zane's eyes. And then the way he'd turned his back and walked away. Just like he'd been doing since she'd shoved him away with her words and denial.

"Well, that's a story that isn't finished," Alice said as she brought Landon over and stood beside her, then looked about at her daughters-in-law and soon-to-be daughter-in-law. It showed that she loved them now as her daughters. "Let's head in that direction. Seth will see us going and will herd the fellas over too. But I have a feeling Tucker isn't going to have to be encouraged to get over here. As far as he's concerned, the wedding could be happening tonight and not tomorrow." She started to walk.

Nina smiled. "You're right. That wonderful cowboy would love tonight to be the night for the wedding. We're all here and there's the preacher stepping up to his spot, ready and waiting."

Lisa watched in wonder as Maggie's eyes lit up, and she stopped walking. Everyone paused to look at her.

Maggie looked around at everyone. "I feel the same way. I'm the one who put this wedding off…but I guess since we planned it for tomorrow and our friends are all coming to the party afterward, we can't do that."

Alice stared at Maggie. "What you said is true. We've got a wonderful group of people from town and surrounding areas who are so excited to celebrate you two getting married. But Maggie, the wedding is private, with just us, the family, so why don't you take a walk over there real quick and talk to your fiancé and see what he says. I have a good feeling I know what he is going to say, but I'm not going to speak for him."

Lisa's heart pounded fiercely with hope and happiness for this sweet woman, who looked suddenly more bright and cheerful than she had a few minutes ago. Her expression was illuminated. *What would it feel like to just give in to your heart like that?* The question tore through her.

"Well, ladies," Maggie said gleefully. "Plans might just be changing." She spun around and headed back down the aisle they'd just walked up.

Tucker, who'd just started walking toward the chairs with the men, saw her and started smiling. He quickly left the men behind and headed her way. Everyone watched as the two met and she began speaking. Though no one could hear her words, a loud hoot erupted from Tucker and a grin swept across his face as he scooped her up into his arms. Her feet were off the ground and her hands on his shoulders as she looked down into his upturned face since she was higher than him now. Her lips came down to meet his with a kiss as he spun them around with clear happiness radiating from them. And then he slowly came to a halt and let her slide down his body. As soon as her feet touched the ground, he cupped her face in his hands and softly said something to her. She was smiling as she nodded and then Tucker spun toward his brothers.

"It's real, guys. We are about to get married now. Not tomorrow. We can celebrate with everyone tomorrow night but right now I'm about to marry this awesome, amazing woman."

The entire group of women and men let out cheers and clapped, and Lisa felt tears trickling from her eyes. She was so happy. In that moment, she realized, as the guys swarmed forward to hug the couple, that Zane had entered the room and stood just behind them and was now in her line of view. Their eyes clung to each other. She fought off her emotions, as hard as it was to do, because this wasn't about her and Zane right now. This was Maggie and Tucker's amazing moment. She did give him a small smile because she didn't want him to think she was being ugly, and then the preacher called them all to come his way and she did.

"This is interesting. I'm here, the license is ready, and it looks like we're about to make these two special people a happily married couple tonight. Tomorrow night, we'll celebrate with everyone but tonight it's just the way it's supposed to be—just a night early but meant to be. So, do we have a bouquet for the bride? And how about rings?"

Sophie waved her arms. "Yes, we have the bouquet. It's in the refrigerator, waiting for tomorrow. The florist got it finished, and I picked it up on my way out tonight. So yes, yes, yes! Let's have a wedding. I'll go get the flowers, and we'll have this beautiful celebration started."

"And the rings are here in my pocket." Tucker reached in and handed them off to Jackson, his best man since Nina was Maggie's matron of honor.

Maggie watched the handoff and laughed in delight. "Yes, here we go." She kissed Tucker quickly, then sprang out of his arms. "I'll wait back here for the bouquet and all my sweet friends. And Seth to give me away because I love him like a father, and my parents are on a Mediterranean cruise and couldn't get a flight in time."

Seth grinned as he stepped forward. "I'm honored and ready."

"Oh, how I love that sweet man." Alice smiled. "This is going to be wonderful. Come sit with me, Lisa. You and that darling baby. Zane," she called. "Come sit in the front with us."

Lisa's gaze flew to Zane; he looked startled but started their way as Seth waved a hand for him to move forward. Lisa spun back around with the baby and followed Alice to the front row with its four chairs. Alice left the far seat open for Seth, and she sat in one of the middle chairs and patted the one beside her. Obviously the one empty one beside her was to be Zane's. As the brothers all gathered to the side of Tucker and all faced the back, their wives lined up with Maggie. Lisa's heart was on a rampage as Zane quietly slid into the seat beside her.

"Za!" Nicky squealed and leaned forward, not letting go of where he had one arm wrapped around her neck.

She had to lean with him as he placed a hand on Zane's jaw. She and Zane were suddenly close as Zane looked at her—mere inches from him.

"Za is a new name for me," he said, his voice a near whisper as his gaze pulled from hers to Nicky. "Hey, little fella, need to let Lisa loose." He reached around the baby, his arm wrapping Nicky and her closer as his fingers touched her neck where he lifted the baby's hand from her.

Lisa would have moved if he'd eased the arm that wrapped around them but he seemed frozen as their gazes locked again. Her heart rumbled rapidly as her gaze shifted to his lips—

"Okay, everyone, let's get this wedding started," the pastor said.

His words slammed into Lisa's heart like an icepick, to a hard, cold, frozen brick of ice.

Zane's gaze penetrated hers, his expression one of alarm. "Are you okay?" he asked quietly, only for her to hear.

"I'm… I'm…" She swallowed hard. *This was not the right time.* "We need to focus on Tucker and

Maggie," she whispered. And then she pulled away, loosening her grip on the baby so he could go to Zane if he wanted. And then she looked straight ahead as her mind whirled with all the things she had to line up and get straight: she loved Zane, and what was about to go on right in front of her as these two married, she wanted to be brave enough to do too.

Zane sat still beside the woman he loved. His heart pounded as he watched each of Seth and Alice's daughters-in-law follow each other up to stand across from their husbands. The preacher lifted his hands as someone in the room who was running the sound system—he wasn't even sure who was doing that—but they shifted the music to the familiar wedding song he'd seen many women walk down the aisle to their groom. He watched Tucker's expression. The man obviously loved the woman about to walk up the short aisle. The preacher looked with a smile about the room. The only people sitting in the chairs were him, Lisa, and Alice, and the two babies. They all stood. He couldn't help himself as he placed a hand on Lisa's lower back and a hand under her arm where the baby sat, hugging her around the neck and grinning at him, as if saying, "I'm not letting her go." Zane felt the same way. He gave her steadiness as she stood; her gaze shifted to his and he felt a sudden jolt as he saw what he thought and hoped was longing. Oh, how he longed for her to long for him.

They were now standing, and he removed his arm, though it took a lot of willpower to do so. But he did it. In his heart of hearts, he felt like something was changing for this beautiful woman standing beside him, holding the baby he loved and longed for her to love and help him raise.

They turned then and watched Seth escorting the bride. The man whose life had changed when he met Alice, just like his had changed when he met Lisa. He watched his good friend escorting his soon-to-be daughter-in-law up the aisle. The beautiful Maggie, who had lost her first love like Alice and Seth, had found new love with Tucker, who had also lost his first love and now found new love with her.

Zane's heart throbbed; he had never found love. Not once, not twice, not at all until he had met Lisa. He smiled as they walked past him, and he turned to face forward. He heard Lisa whisper something softly to the baby, who had started chattering. The baby quieted; Lisa had a way with that baby. She would have been a wonderful mother and he prayed in that moment as the preacher asked, "Who is giving the bride away?"

Seth said he was and the couple offered their hands out in front of them. Maggie took Tucker's hand; she passed the beautiful flowers she carried to Nina and then she locked gazes with Tucker, and he with her.

It was a beautiful scene, full of emotion, and Zane couldn't help himself as his head turned slightly and he realized that she was looking at him. He swallowed hard, his lips lifting into a cautious smile, and her face softened as she gave him a gentle, closed-lip smile as her eyes moistened with emotion. He and she both then yanked their gazes apart as the preacher started the wedding vows.

His heart thundered and, in that moment, he focused in on this wonderful moment as Maggie and

Tucker gazed at each other and the preacher spoke the words that would make them become one.

And he prayed that he and Lisa could do the same.

~*~

Maggie was ecstatic as Tucker looked into her eyes, smiling as the preacher announced them husband and wife. She burst into a smile, and he and she met in a kiss that she would never forget. He swept her into his arms as his lips and hers joined as if saying *Yes, we are now one together*, and she prayed that they had a long life together. She trembled with joy and excitement, and the kiss lasted and she could hear everyone around them sending shouts of joy for them.

Tucker eased up and, with his lips almost touching her, he smiled. "I love you, Maggie McIntyre, and am blessed you love me."

She leaned her head back just enough to look into his eyes. "I feel the same, Tucker."

They kissed one more swift kiss, then he took her hand and they spun toward everyone as he held her hand in the air, wedding ring shining in the lights. "All I can say is never give up on love. Never."

Maggie was smiling ear to ear as she so agreed and, in that moment, her happy gaze landed on two smiling people standing beside each other with a precious baby clapping excitedly. *This could be them if they gave in to what was between them.* But that was not what she was focused on right now; it was that she had given in to what was between her and Tucker, and she was so very glad. Maybe soon they would be standing beside each other, holding their baby, their treasure, and be very aware of the blessing that had been bestowed on them.

CHAPTER FIFTEEN

Tucker was ecstatic as he'd announced that he and this wonderful love of his life were now husband and wife. He scanned his family and saw how thrilled they were, and he also caught Zane's eyes as he stood there beside Lisa, who was holding Nicky. Tucker so wanted them to be together but that wasn't up to him. All he could do was be grateful that his life now had a happy ending and say a prayer that Zane's would too. And now it was time to celebrate.

"Let's celebrate early, everybody. Tonight, and tomorrow night, because as far as I'm concerned, this is worth two nights of celebration. And there is no one I'd rather do it with than all of you and this beautiful lady. So come on, let's eat. Let's have a great evening, and then I'm going to take this pretty lady home—well, to one of our homes tonight, whichever one she chooses." He looked at her and chuckled. "We have my cabin here on the ranch and her home with the pretty ocean view. I think we'll keep them."

Everyone cheered and she smiled up at him. "I agree. Nothing like having a getaway so close together. But tonight we'll go to your cabin since those two cabins were how we came to know each other."

His mother came up, beaming, and hugged him tightly. Seth stood beside her and Dallas, now holding Landon with his other arm around Lorna, stood behind their mom. Alice's arms were empty now, which enabled her to reach for Maggie and draw her into the hug. A grinning Seth joined in, throwing an arm around Alice and the other around the newly married couple.

Tucker loved it.

"I am so very glad," his mom said. "What a wonderful turn of events. You two are going to have a wonderful life. Just like me and this man right here are having. You two will be so happy."

"And I agree with her," Seth added. "We are here

for you two, but I have a feeling y'all have it handled. You are both solid in your love and plans, and I'm just going to say go for it, enjoy this new life you've joined together to share."

"I agree with Mom and Seth," Dallas said, smiling at Lorna. "Life is an adventure, and I'm loving every moment that this amazing woman and I joined together to share. And we are excited that you two are about to do the same."

"Yes, we are," Lorna added. "I'm loving every moment of ours, and I know you two will also."

All of his brothers and sisters-in-law swarmed them. Then, after all of them had congratulated them, he squeezed Maggie's hand as he saw Zane and Lisa approaching them together. Zane was now holding the baby, but they came together and that was a good sign. He knew Maggie agreed as she squeezed his hand tightly and gave it a little shake. He understood that was her show of excitement that maybe, just maybe as she'd hoped tonight, their night might have shone a spotlight on what their hopes were for these two awesome, deserving people.

"Congratulations, you two," Zane said, with a large smile. "It was perfect, and I wish you a wonderful life. I know there are a lot of words but wonderful is just the word that fits for me right now."

"And I agree." Lisa smiled as she reached out and hugged Maggie and then him. "You two are just wonderful together…" She laughed softly. "I guess you see how much I agree, since that's the word that comes forward for me too."

They all chuckled together happily, and Maggie caught Tucker's eyes. He saw the hope in her beautiful eyes for these two. "We are really glad you came, and Zane, thanks for bringing that baby because he helped lead us together quicker than what could have been. He's a blessing, and I send my thanks to his parents for sending him here. Though I am so sorry they aren't here to celebrate with us in person. However, I feel that they are here in spirit and happy to see how well he is being loved."

Zane looked at the baby. "I love him dearly and yes, he is a huge blessing. And I can tell you that Dave and Becca are smiling down right now. They are happy that he helped you two out. And also, happy that their precious baby is so loved here by all of us." His gaze went to Lisa.

Tucker smiled hugely, his heart throbbing as he met Maggie's gaze. She was beaming, too.

"We are hoping and planning that we can give Nicky a playmate in the near future, maybe a year or hopefully by a year and a half. Soon is what we want."

Lisa gasped, excitement in her gasp. "That is so wonderful. You two will be amazing parents, and just keep me in mind for a babysitter. I'm going to slow down in my hours since I have such great help with my two wonderful backups. I had another great backup but he has a wonderful job taking care of this delightful baby, but I will be hoping to get to babysit for you two."

Tucker did not miss the look Zane had flash in his eyes when he looked from him to the ground.

"You can count on it," Maggie said. "We'll have you at the top of the list. You, like me—at least, I like to think I do—deserve a baby of your own. And if you don't end up with that, then I hope my baby and all of my nephews and nieces I'm expecting we are going to have can help fill that spot."

Maggie reached out and hugged Lisa again.

Tucker and Zane's gazes met over their heads, and Tucker could not help it; he mouthed the silent words: "*Go for it.*"

~*~

After the moments they'd spent there with the newlyweds, Zane and Lisa had separated as the dinner got going. He had kept the baby with him because he could tell Nicky was getting tired. Zane's heart was racing, his thoughts swerving in and out on what his next step would be. He wanted to walk over there right now, bow down in front of her as he held this baby and ask her to please marry him. But he wouldn't do that.

He knew that she was vulnerable right now and as much as he wanted to ask her, as much as he wanted her in his life, he couldn't take advantage of her obvious weak moment. When he did ask her, he wanted it to be their moment. And if she turned him down, he wasn't sure if he'd keep trying until she threatened to hurt him if he didn't leave her alone. He hoped he didn't have to make that decision. He prayed that what he saw in her expressions tonight wouldn't just be from the emotions of this wedding. That they would be true, and things would be what he felt they were supposed to be. That they would get their happily ever after.

Everyone was having a great time, so happy for Tucker and Maggie. After an hour, he knew it was time to head home and put this little fella in bed. He walked over to Seth, who he'd ridden out to the ranch with, not having realized all the early celebrating that was coming. "Thanks for the ride out, and since your sweet wife is here, would it be a problem if I took your truck and headed home? It's time to put Nicky to bed. It's been a great, awesome night."

Seth grinned. "Yeah, you can say that again. Keys are in it. I'll call you tomorrow before I walk over and grab it. Drive safe. And, Zane, you looked good standing there with that awe-inspiring woman standing beside you, holding that baby during the ceremony. Good luck. Go for it. We're all rooting for you, man."

Zane clapped a hand on his friend's arms. "Thanks.

I need it. I just have to figure out the right time to go for it."

"Well, do it," Seth said, smiling like the sun had just blown up inside him. "You'll figure out the right time."

He told Seth to let everyone know that he and baby were sneaking out but he would be at the party the next night. Then he took his baby—*his baby.* His heart squeezed tight around those words. Dave and Becca had gifted their son to him so that he would raise him with their love but also his love. And he was doing that, and he accepted that he'd called sweet Nicky his boy.

He got in the truck and by the time he'd made the drive from the ranch to his place by the ocean, Nicky was sound asleep in his car seat. Zane was very careful as he got him out and entered the house. He walked down the hallway and into Nicky's room, where he lowered him into his bed. Slowly he eased his clothes off and changed his diaper, and the baby continued to sleep, with a slight smile to his lips. That touch of a smile dug deep into Zane. He put the sleeper on, then pulled a light blanket over him. He backed up to the door and continued to stare at the soft breathing, content baby. Then he turned and headed down the hallway to the kitchen.

Feeling twisted and anxious, he opened the refrigerator and pulled out a container of orange juice. He shook it and poured some into a glass. He didn't hardly ever drink alcohol but right now he needed something strong and tangy, and the orange juice was exactly that. He needed something to zap him into reality as he headed out onto the back porch. He sat on a chair and stared out at the moonlit bay and wondered what his next step should be. He was sitting there a little while later when he heard a vehicle pull into his driveway.

He looked at his watch. It was now ten o'clock. *Had Seth decided to come now and get his truck?* He set his juice down and stood and headed from the patio toward the carport to see who was there. He was about to round the corner when Lisa appeared in the pale moonlight. He froze. His heart went crazy and then stilled like the rest of him as they stared at each other.

He was speechless. No words would come out.

Lisa cupped her hands together in front of her stomach as she took a step forward. "I hope this isn't a bad time. I started going home and passed my road and came here. I couldn't stop myself. Zane, tonight was eye-opening and heart-opening for me." She held her hand up when he started to speak. "I need to say this, please."

He nodded and kept his mouth shut, hoping and praying that what she was about to say was something he wanted to hear. Hoped to hear.

"I was scared. I had been done wrong, and I had been letting that wrong moment in my life dictate the rest of my life. And then you entered my life and despite what I was feeling, I continued to try to let the dictation continue, trying so hard despite what being near you, around you, and in your arms filled me with. I was in denial. I was so afraid and I was judging you where I shouldn't have. And tonight…"

A soft, gentle smile lifted her lips. "Tonight, I knew I can't deny myself happiness with you anymore, if you still want me. I was being ridiculous, letting that man dictate my life instead of standing strong and going after what I wanted. And what I want is you and that sweet boy. But even if that sweet boy wasn't in your life, I would still want you, Zane. You have filled me with hope and joy that I've been denying, and I'm here now, asking if you still feel that way?"

Zane was breaking up inside with happiness and she was wondering whether he still felt that way, in wanting her in his life? In four steps, he crossed to her, took her face between his palms, and looked into her beautiful, soft green eyes and felt his own dampening. "I love you, Lisa, and I will always cherish you. You are the only love I've ever had, wanted, or ever will have."

And then, as tears rolled from her eyes, he kissed her. His lips covered hers; his heart radiated as she wrapped her arms around him and held on tight. Every ounce of his being released to her in that kiss, that mingling of love as he dug deep and she joined in.

Life was about to start at last. And he was more than ready to enjoy every moment spent with the lady he loved so very deeply.

"I've waited all my life for you, Lisa, and you're worth every moment spent waiting for you and no other."

"I love you, and am so ready for our life together as husband and wife and parents to sweet Nicky to begin."

"We're going to make his mom and dad proud. I can hear them cheering us on." And it was true. He knew those two loving people were happy right now, knowing he had this wonderful woman ready to give their baby her love, her heart like she was giving him. This was what true love looked like, and he could feel it deeply as he smiled, looking into her soft green eyes that sparkled with true love.

CHAPTER SIXTEEN

We're having a wedding!

It was fabulous news, and Zane wanted to declare it to everyone, as did Lisa, but she couldn't. They could not take the shine from Tucker and Maggie's special celebration, so they decided to let everyone know on Sunday or Monday. Neither of them wanted to wait to get married. They agreed that they'd both waited their lifetime for this moment and didn't want to put it off. They would file on Monday morning for a marriage license and the wedding would be Thursday evening. But they weren't telling anyone until after Tucker and Maggie had their night of celebration. But they couldn't not go, so they chose to ride together, get there a bit late so no one would see them arrive together and maybe just think they'd walked in at the same time. It was a little lame, she had to admit, but she hadn't been able to not ride with him.

So, here they were, the two happiest people in the world and the sweetest baby in Zane's arms as they entered the tent. It was going to be so hard to pretend that they didn't have exciting news. Lisa wanted more than anything to share this with Alice, but she wouldn't tonight. Tomorrow was soon enough. They didn't want to take anything away from beautiful Maggie and amazing Tucker's wedding. But as strange as it was, the first two people they saw as they walked into the tent was the wedding couple.

Maggie stared at her and then at Tucker, as a huge smile burst across her face. She elbowed Tucker in the ribs, but he was already grinning at them too.

They rushed toward them and Lisa just stood there, fighting back a huge grin of happiness that matched Maggie's.

"You two look so very happy tonight," Maggie crooned. "Is there something going on that would make my day any more wonderful?"

Lisa stared into this young woman's eyes, who had been through so much, and she knew that Maggie had figured it all out, as had Tucker. She glanced at Zane, and he was smiling, knowing the secret was obviously on their own faces, so she took Maggie's hands. "I didn't want to take anything from your beautiful, special night. But from the way you're looking and the way you're acting, I think, if I'm not completely wrong, that I'm about to give you an unusual wedding gift. Zane and I had a long talk last night, and we are getting married on Thursday night and would love for you two to come."

Maggie let out a squeal that alerted the entire crowd that something fantastic had just been announced. She sealed the deal by throwing her arms around Lisa's neck and hugging her tight. Tucker did the same to Zane, who was holding the baby she loved dearly too.

Then Tucker turned toward the watchful group and Maggie did the same, still holding onto Lisa. "Everyone, we don't just have one wonderful wedding to celebrate tonight. We also have an upcoming wedding to celebrate. I guess you don't mind if I told everyone?" he asked with a grin.

Zane laughed and wrapped the arm not holding Nicky around her shoulders and pulled her close, looking deep into her eyes—almost making her faint, looking at the love shining there. "No, I don't mind. I love this woman and have since the first moment I set foot in her office. She made my life a dream come true when she agreed to marry me last night. So yes, if you don't mind, we'll celebrate with you tonight and then again with just a small gathering at her house on Thursday night when she becomes my wife."

Everyone cheered, and immediately Alice came running and threw her arms around Lisa. She hugged her so tight, swaying them back and forth, and then she leaned back with tears in her eyes. "I am so, so happy. Why did you not call me and warn me? I'm going to be crying with happiness all night now."

Lisa laughed as tears rolled down her face. "I just didn't want to take away the happiness for these two wonderful people standing beside us."

"You're not taking it away," Maggie declared. "Tucker and I had been hoping our wedding would help bring this on the whole time. So you two have gifted us with the most wonderful gift you could have given us.

And see, my new mother-in-law is so happy, it's just icing on a very thick icing-coated cake. The moment I married that handsome man right there—and I know my sisters-in-law will say the same thing and probably my brothers-in-law—life has a new meaning."

"She's right about that." Jackson came up and shook hands with Zane, followed by Riley, Dallas, and Seth.

And she, while he was being congratulated, was embraced in a massive hug by Maggie, Sophie, Lorna, Nina, and Alice. They hugged her at the same time and they cheered.

And Lisa knew in that beautiful moment that absolutely all or more than she could have ever dreamed had come true. She had a family, a large, wonderful family now, and all of those dreams had come true. As she wiped tears from her eyes and smiled at everyone, she knew as her gaze met Zane's teary eyes that they were now going to make new dreams come true.

She had gone through heartbreak, disaster, and then watched everybody else get a happy ever after and now here she stood, having her own. And feeling so very blessed that she had come to her senses and opened her heart again. And not let a first bad impression hold her back for the rest of her life.

She reached out and took that sweet baby who was waving his arms at her into her arms and kissed his small forehead. He wrapped his tiny arm around her neck as if he'd watched everyone else hugging her and now he was going to get his hug. Then he leaned back and looked at her, his palm on her jaw.

His eyes grew bright. "Maawma, maaa, ma. Mama." The words came out, staggered and stuttered, but his eyes told her that he knew what he was saying. He wanted her too.

Zane stepped forward and wrapped his arms around both of them. "Yes, little fella. This is going to be your new mama. Although I'm going to bring you up as my little son, we're also going to teach you about your real loving mom and daddy. We're going to love you like we love each other, like no one else could do."

Everyone was wiping tears from their eyes and smiling when Lisa lifted her tearful eyes from Zane's shoulder and their gazes locked. Oh happy day...*this* was what true love was made of and she was so blessed to have found him.

EPILOGUE

Lisa looked across the room to where Alice stood in the center of her and Seth's living room. Her good friend smiled as she gazed around the small area. "The house is beautifully decorated for Christmas," Lisa said and meant it.

She had also decorated her and Zane's house and loved it too. They'd both begun working at the inn together and taking turns staying home with sweet Nicky and making the house into a home. She loved it and loved her new life just as much as Alice loved hers. They'd both been blessed and we not taking it for granted.

Alice locked her hands together beneath her chin and her eyebrows dipped. "I so love it. But, compared to the living room at the ranch where we used to have Christmas with the family, it's going to be a bit of a tight squeeze. But this is mine and Seth's first Christmas and I told the kids I wanted to have Christmas day here, and they all agreed wholeheartedly. Isn't that sweet."

"They love Seth and are so happy you found him."

"Yes, they are. They do love him so. As much as they loved their amazing father, they are more than happy that I found Seth. And," she smiled at Lisa, who was sitting on the edge of the couch watching Nicky as he sat on the rug playing with the tiny stuffed seahorse he was holding in his hand and the firetruck he was rolling with his other hand. "I'm so glad you and Zane agreed to celebrate Christmas with us. Nicky is so adorable, and little Landon is going to probably plop down right there with him and play."

"I'll love him playing with Nicky. I just know he and Landon will be wonderful friends. And also, I'll love the two new babies you'll be welcoming soon. Does Lorna have a date to enter the hospital if she doesn't go into labor soon?" They were all anticipating the birth of Lorna and Dallas's baby, Landon's new sister, who was running a bit late of her arrival date. And then, of course, Nina was due any day too.

"She's right at a week and a half late of her due date so she's set to enter the hospital to be induced on Tuesday. Since it's Friday and Christmas Day I used it as another reason for having the celebration here. Just in case Lorna goes into labor this will make the hospital a whole lot closer than the ranch."

Lisa smiled hugely. "Do you think it could be today? That would be a great Christmas present to you. To everyone."

"Oh, yes it would be." Alice chuckled and glanced out the window at Seth and Zane standing at the outdoor deep fryer getting ready to cook the Christmas turkey. They were talking and laughing, and Lisa was so grateful her new and loving husband Zane was such a great friend with Alice's husband. "I'm so glad they are such good friends. God did good by us, didn't He?"

A smile exploded across Lisa's face. "Yes, in so many wonderful and touching ways." Her gaze went to the baby.

"Lisa, what a blessing you are to that sweet boy and

that wonderful man out there," Alice said softly.

Tears of happiness threatened Lisa because she felt so strongly blessed. "My heart is so full these days, Alice. I'm so thankful and happy."

"Me too. And with these new babies coming it's going to be so delightful. Lisa, we are going to have a complete herd of babies to enjoy."

"Yes, we are—"

They both laughed just as the front door opened. "Knock knock," Jackson called as he stepped inside, holding the door as he helped his very pregnant wife enter. "I've brought my jewels to visit."

Nina smiled at him, though she looked tired, and since she was due in a week and a half, it was understandable. "I'm glad to be here but I will warn you all that I'll be shocked if I make it to my due date." She sank into the chair closest to the door.

Alice glanced at Lisa with a worried expression, then hurried over and knelt down in front of Nina. "Are you hurting?"

Jackson rested a hand on Nina's shoulder. "She was earlier but is better."

"I'm fine, just tired," Nina gave a weak smile at Alice. "But I keep thinking what a great Christmas present this little fella would be for all of us if he decided to come today."

"What would be a great Christmas present?" Tucker asked as he and Maggie came inside holding hands.

"Babies being born." Alice grinned at them. "So glad y'all are here. Nina is hurting, might be going into labor."

"Awesome," Maggie exclaimed, looking with bright eyes at Tucker and then to Nina. "This is wonderful."

"What's wonderful?" Dallas asked as he and Lorna entered the still open door. He too had his wife's arm linked through his as they came across the room and he held her steady as she sank to the couch.

Riley and Sophie followed with a toddling Landon between them. They must have driven up at the same time and took over the boy so Dallas could help Lorna.

"These two babies," Alice exclaimed, smiling from her kneeling position to her other expecting daughter-in-law. Nina is ready, how about you, Lorna?" She threw her arms open wide as Landon broke loose and flung himself at his grandma. "Hey sweet fella."

Lorna smiled, watching her boy love his grandmother. She had a hand on her round tummy. "I'm so ready. Tuesday can't get here fast enough. I've had some Braxton Hicks pains the last couple of days, so I'm hoping the real ones start soon."

"She's staying off the beach this time," Dallas said with a smile. "We might have met on the beach when she went into labor with Landon but we'd rather this little one come into the world inside the hospital."

Landon had gotten his hugs from Alice and now his gaze locked on Nicky as Lisa sat him up in her lap. She smiled at the way Landon's eyes widened and he rushed over to give his new friend a hug. "Hey, Landon. Nicky is glad to see you too." She would distract the boys as the family shared their thoughts about the new babies.

"Nicky, play?" he asked taking Nicky's hand as if to walk away with him.

"Yes, let's get down here on the floor and pull out some toys." She slid from the chair to the rug and reached for the bag of toys, stuffed zebra, and rolling plastic trucks. And a horse that Landon instantly reached for.

"Horse race," he said and made the hand-sized horse gallop along the rug. Everyone laughed, and Lisa did too.

"Oh!" Lorna gasped drawing everyone's gaze. It was such a sharp sound, and her expression was one of pain.

Dallas instantly squatted down in front of her. "Honey, you okay?"

She flinched again. "I-I think this is real." Her pain-filled eyes flashed with pain and excitement. "Dallas, we're having a baby."

"Awesome!" Dallas exclaimed and jumped to his feet.

"What's up?" Seth asked coming in the back door with Zane following him.

"We're having a baby," Alice squealed as she too jumped up just as Nina groaned, drawing attention from Lorna to her.

"Nina, are you okay?" Jackson asked, moving from

behind her to the front so he could look at her grimacing expression.

"I think I'm in labor too."

"Oh my goodness," Alice exclaimed, looking from Lorna to Nina. "Come on, everyone, let's get these sweet gals to the hospital. What a Christmas gift today is."

Zane came instantly to Lisa's side and reached down and took Nicky from her lap and gave her a hand to help her up.

An excited Sophie lifted her nephew into her arms. "This is wonderful," Sophie said, grinning at Landon. "You're about to be a big brother, little fella."

Zane was grinning as he looked at Lisa. "This is going to be a great day. Come on, everyone, let's head out."

"Alice," Seth called as he opened the back door. "Get your things and I'll turn off the turkey cooker and meet you at the truck."

"Great that you remembered the turkey fryer," Zane chuckled as his friend closed the door and jogged out to the tall steel pot on top of the gas grill.

Lisa and Zane held back as they let everyone walk outside ahead of them. They paused in the yard and watched the expecting dads help their wives into the trucks. Zane had his arm around her shoulders and kissed the top of her head. "You ready to go to the house and get in our truck?"

They had just walked over because they knew there would be several trucks in the drive. "I'm ready. What a wonderful day."

He chuckled as one by one the trucks backed out and headed down the street. Seth hurried from the backyard toward his truck which now had room to back out. "Y'all can ride with us," he called as Alice rolled her window down.

"Yes, come on and ride with us."

"No, y'all go ahead," Zane said. "We'll grab things for Nicky and then buckle him into his car seat and meet y'all at the hospital."

"Right, car seats. I've got to get me some more," Alice said, grinning. "This is so exciting."

Lisa laughed. "Yes, it is. Now go. We'll be there soon."

They watched their joyous friends back out and then head down the street, following their family. Lisa looked up at Zane, her heart pounding with love. "I'm so excited for them and so very happy to have you and Nicky by my side."

He grinned down at her then planted a wonderful kiss to her lips. "No happier than I am to have you in my arms and heart. Now, come on. Let's go welcome these new babies into the world."

Hand in hand, they hurried the short distance to their home, and he strapped Nicky into his car seat while she hurried inside to get what the baby would need while they waited. This was a wonderful Christmas. She was now a happily married woman and a mother to a sweet baby boy and now getting to enjoy all of her friends having babies. She might not have gotten to go through labor and bring her own baby into the world, but that was okay because she loved little Nicky with all of her heart and was just so blessed to be his mom. To share that with Becca, whom she'd come to know through everything Zane had told her about Nicky's deceased mother and his daddy too. She would always let the little fella know he was loved here on earth and from heaven above.

She hurried outside to the now running truck and set the baby bag in the back seat, and then climbed into the front seat. She strapped into her seatbelt and Zane backed them out of the drive and then headed after the line of trucks that were now out of view. Soon they were at the hospital and up the elevator to the second floor, and the waiting room where Seth, Alice, Sophie and Riley were waiting and the soon-to-be daddies were in the back with their wives.

Dear Alice had Landon in her arms and looked overjoyed as her gaze locked with Lisa's.

"They're already back there getting prepared," Riley said, grinning hugely. His gaze went from theirs to Sophie, who Lisa realized was smiling deeply and her pretty eyes were almost dancing with excitement.

"We're so happy to get to come spend this exciting day with all of you," Lisa said and meant it.

And so the wait began and though they expected to wait for hours if need be they were shocked when less than an hour later Dallas came busting from the double doors grinning. "She's here! Beautiful little sweetie cuddling with her mamma." He was all smiles as he beamed at them.

"Oh, I can't wait to hold her," Alice said, tears shining in her eyes.

Suddenly Jackson came bounding out the double doors. "Okay, everyone, William McIntyre the second is born." His expression was full of joy as he met his mom's eyes.

"You named him after your dad," she said, her voice shaking. "Oh, Jackson, he is smiling down right now." Alice took Jackson's hand and Dallas's hand in each of hers. "Your father is thrilled and so am I, and Seth too. What a wonderful, wonderful gift today is."

Zane stood behind Lisa as she held the baby but at the news, he placed his arms around her and Nicky and rested his mouth beside her ear. "What a great day."

She turned her head and kissed his jaw. "I'm so happy." But if she thought this great day couldn't be any better, a grinning Riley and Sophie stepped up their gazed locking with Tucker and Maggie, who were also grinning.

"Mom, we all have some more news to add to this great day," Riley said.

"Yes, we do," Tucker added. "We talked about it and decided we might as well add to the happiness of the day."

The two couples were beaming at Alice now, and Lisa's heart began to explode with more joy as she realized her friend was about to have more good news added to this amazing day.

"We're expecting too," Riley and Sophie, Maggie and Tucker all said together.

Instantly laughter and joy erupted among everyone. "Oh, what a wonderful, wonderful day," Alice said, tears streaming down her face. "I'm the happiest woman alive."

Lisa felt such love for her sweet friend and her family and snuggled against the body of Zane as his arms tightened around her. "She's so blessed," Lisa whispered against Zane's skin. "But Zane, I'm just as blessed. I love you so and this sweet boy is going to have a bundle of wonderful friends and family to grow up around."

He kissed her cheek. "I feel the same way. What a wonderful life we're going to have. I love you so much, Lisa."

"And I feel the same. Now, let's go celebrate, sharing these hugs of happiness with our friends. Oh, what a happy, happy new year this is going to be. Well, it's started already, a wonderful ending to this year and fabulous new beginning for all of us."

"Amen, to that," Zane said, and together they went to join in on the celebrating with their friends—their family.

Oh, what a wonderful life had begun for all of them.

More Books by Debra Clopton

Star Gazer Inn of Corpus Christi Bay
What New Beginnings are Made of (Book 1)
What Dreams are Made of (Book 2)
What Hopes are Made of (Book 3)
What a Heart's Desire is Made of (Book 4)
What True Love is Made of (Book 5)

Check out Debra's Other Series
Sunset Bay Romance
Texas Brides & Bachelors
New Horizon Ranch Series
Turner Creek Ranch Series
Cowboys of Ransom Creek
Texas Matchmaker Series
Windswept Bay Series

About the Author

Debra Clopton is a USA Today bestselling & International bestselling author who has sold over 3.5 million books. She has published over 81 books under her name and her pen name of Hope Moore.

Under both names she writes clean & wholesome and inspirational, small town romances, especially with cowboys but also loves to sweep readers away with romances set on beautiful beaches surrounded by topaz water and romantic sunsets.

Her books now sell worldwide and are regulars on the Bestseller list in the United States and around the world. Debra is a multiple award-winning author, but of all her awards, it is her reader's praise she values most. If she can make someone smile and forget their worries for a few hours (or days when binge reading one of her series) then she's done her job and her heart is happy. She really loves hearing she kept a reader from doing the dishes or sleeping!

A sixth-generation Texan, Debra lives on a ranch in Texas with her husband surrounded by cattle, deer, very busy squirrels and hole digging wild hogs. She enjoys traveling and spending time with her family.

Visit Debra's website and sign up for her newsletter
for updates at: www.debraclopton.com

Check out her Facebook at:
www.facebook.com/debra.clopton.5

Follow her on Instagram at: debraclopton_author

or contact her at debraclopton@ymail.com